KU-662-485

GOLD ON THE HOOF

Most people in Wagonspoke view old Fred Locke's Broken Key Ranch as a downgrade, white elephant spread. Once a lush cattle kingdom in eastern California's Verde Valley, its water-starved range is now to be delivered into the hands of the bank.

Kyle Kruze owns the bank and runs it, along with many other enterprises, from the casino across the street. Kruze lived by violence alone until he met Cloyd Weber, whose shrewd manipulation of the law gives their operations a thin front of legitimacy.

With the death of Fred Locke, one man with clenched fists stands against these two. Tuck Clayburn, foreman of Broken Key, knows that the ranch is worth saving. And then there is his beautiful daughter Randie—reason enough.

GOLD ON THE HOOF

Walker A. Tompkins

GUNSMOKE

First published in the UK by Wright and Brown

This hardback edition 2008
by BBC Audiobooks Ltd
by arrangement with
Golden West Literary Agency

Copyright © 1953 by Walker A. Tompkins.
Copyright © 1953 by Walker A. Tompkins in
the British Commonwealth.
Copyright © renewed 1981 by Walker A. Tompkins.
All rights reserved.

ISBN 978 1 405 68169 8

British Library Cataloguing in Publication Data available.

KENT LIBRARIES AND ARCHIVES	
C153345566	
HJ	19/02/2008
	£9.95

Printed and bound in Great Britain by
Antony Rowe Ltd., Chippenham, Wiltshire

for

LURANA • EILEEN • LES

Gold on the Hoof

chapter 1

In the shade of the lacy tamaracks behind
the Wagonspoke jailhouse somebody fired a gun to cele-
brate tossing the winning ringer in a high stakes horseshoe
game. The shot breached the siesta quiet that enveloped the
cowtown, startling citizens out of the lethargy of the summer swelter, and flushing a dark cloud of ravens from the
compost pile beside the Wells Fargo barn.

From the window of Dr. Ashton's office on Main Street,
Fred Locke watched the birds dip and zoom against the
shimmering saffron sky, spiral briefly over Kruze's brick
saloon, then settle on the telegraph wires in front of the
assay office, arranging themselves like so many quarter-notes
on a musical staff.

Something about the birds put a poignant stab in the old
cattle king's throat. It puzzled him, until he realized what
the freedom of those ravens symbolized to him. All his life,
he had been as unshackled as they. Now he was waiting for
Doc Ashton to speak the verdict which would close the
book.

Across a span of forty turbulent frontier years, whenever
Fred Locke came down to Wagonspoke from his Broken

Key citadel in the mountains, he always had dropped in on Doc for a social call. This morning was different. Death sat at his elbow. Waiting——

He and Doc had arrived together in Verde Valley, on California's arid eastern border, as boys. This place had been just a water hole then. A yellow wagonspoke stuck in a sand dune identified it for the skinners of twenty-mule teams freighting crude borax out of Death Valley and ore from Cerro Gordo.

Growing up, Fred and Doc had watched this settlement take root and thrive, first as a freighter's camp, later as the outfitting point for the Highgrade gold rush of the sixties, and finally as the supply base for cattlemen and the seat of Indio County's government.

"Tuck Clayburn with you?" Doc Ashton inquired, exploring Locke's ribs with the bell of his stethoscope, making conversation, keeping his patient's mind occupied with other things.

"Tuck and old Tweedy rode out this mornin' on a week's scout of my Lavastone Range," Locke murmured, his eyes still on the quarreling ravens on the telegraph wires. "Countin' buzzard-picked carcasses instead of tallyin' beef critters. I'll know how bad off Broken Key is when they git back."

Doc Ashton clicked his tongue. "These California droughts run in seven-year cycles, the almanac says."

"Then we got three more dry years to go. I won't have a critter left by then, not countin' Randie's little jag up at Summer Range. It's green as a ten-cent gold ring up there."

They lapsed into silence, both trying not to think about how unusual this visit of Fred's was. Not once in four

10

decades had Locke needed Ashton's professional help. Now it was too late.

The view from Doc's window on the second floor of the Cattlemen's Bank Building was one of Fred's special favorites. It was not as sweeping as the one from the porch of his own ranch house, two thousand feet higher up on a bench facing out from the Lavastone foothills, but it had been the setting for several of his life's more memorable events.

From where he sat beside Doc's examination table, he could see the narrow slot in the Furnace Range marking Wagongap Pass, from whose summit he and Doc had first glimpsed this valley.

Framed squarely in the center of the window, a block away, stood the curly-shingled, lightning-rodded steeple of the old Federated Church, where Fred and Molly had been married long ago. In that same church, a quarter-century later, he had looked down on Molly's face in her coffin; a week after that had seen the baptism of Randie, the baby girl God had given them after so many childless years.

By raising up a little in his chair, Locke could see the bullet hole in the false front of the post office, put there by Kyle Kruze the gambler. The bullet had been intended for Locke's ribs but Kruze's aim had been deflected by a .45 slug from Locke's Colt. His one and only gun brawl——

By now, Fred and Doc had become living legends in this frontier land. They had seen the coming of barbwire to Verde Valley and the building of the telegraph line over Wagongap Pass. What changes they had witnessed were all man-made, and would pass away with the erosion of time; but the mountain heights and the desert sinks, the

11

roundabout prairies and conifer-scented canyons of the Lavastones and the Furnaces were eternal, a man's monument after he was gone.

The ravens burst away from the telegraph wires out front, scattered by an incoming stagecoach from Independence, and the racket they made startled Fred Locke out of his reverie.

"You're takin' an infernal long time checkin' me, Doc."

Ashton stopped pumping air into the rubber bandage knotted around Locke's sinewy arm. He detached the blood-pressure apparatus, unhooked the stethoscope plugs from his ears, and said on an exhaled breath, "You can put your shirt back on now."

It wasn't easy to tell a friend of half a century's standing that any breath might be his last, that his whang-leather constitution had played out prematurely. Fred Locke hadn't known an hour's sickness in the sixty-odd years of his vigorous life. Out here, men took it for granted they would live to crowd ninety, barring accident. A good share of them did.

The rancher sensed the verdict in the way Doc Ashton avoided looking at him, making an unnecessary amount of fuss stowing away his instruments. So he made it easy for Doc.

"I'm goin' to sack my saddle ahead of my time, eh, pard?"

The cowtown medico slumped into his swivel chair, heart heavy. He had attended Locke's parents in their last days; he had delivered baby Randie and a week later had prepared for burial the mother who had conceived too late in life. Now his professional services had come full circle

12

through a second generation. He knew Fred would want it straight, without beating around the bush.

"Angina. And your arteries are as stiff as bobwire."

"That's bad?"

"Bad enough I'm surprised you made it upstairs, Fred."

Locke finished buttoning up his hickory shirt, tucking the tails under his shell-belted bibless levis. He murmured, "Thanks, Doc," and, squaring his shoulders, walked over to the window, open wide on this sultry June day.

Moisture blurred Fred's vision, dimming the familiar picture of Wagonspoke's dusty street, which he had helped lay out. It was wide enough for a twenty-mule jerkline string to turn a pair of tandem-hitched wagons between plank sidewalks with room to spare.

He had seen all these deadfalls and honkeytonks go up, their unpainted false fronts rubbing shoulders on both sides of Main.

During the years Locke had been building Broken Key into one of the largest working ranches in California, he had made a sideline of hauling some of the lumber that had gone into these buildings. Every shack, every alley, every hitching post told a nostalgic story to him.

The new gilt lettering on the shingle of Cloyd Weber's law office above the gambling hall flashed in the sun, catching Locke's eye and reminding him bitterly of the bad luck that name had brought into his life. Or unhappiness, rather. A man shaped his own luck. You didn't have much to say about your only daughter being attracted to the wrong man.

"How long would you say, Doc?"

As he spoke Fred stared at the Furnace Mountains, tracing the inverted Y of the Anviliron River's parallel forking

13

canyons on either side of the ridge where the old Borax Road ran down from the Pass. Mountains were fixed, permanent, aloof from man's petty scratchings and bickerings and physical decay; now they gave him comfort in the hardest moment he had ever weathered.

Paul Ashton lifted his gnarled hands from his knees, let them drop back.

"Try tossin' a forty-pound saddle onto a horse and you'll snuff out like a candle. Stay in bed around the clock and you ought to hold out to see Randie get married next April."

Well, that was it. Fred had loved life, every lusty, embattled hour of it. Even of late years, when repeated seasons without rain or snow had swept his proud brand to the brink of bankruptcy, when only the benevolence of Clem Moon, the banker downstairs, had kept Broken Key from foundering, he still loved life.

"She's been a good fling while she lasted," Fred observed, fingering the staghorn butt of the old Army .45 slung at his hip. "Hell of it is, Doc, I ain't ready to go. I'd counted on hitting eighty before I even began to slow up. I'm leavin' my affairs too muddled."

The doctor murmured, "Same way with everybody, Fred, when their turn comes. Only most folks don't get advance warnin' so they can put their houses in order and prepare to meet their Maker."

Locke turned away from the window, grinning.

"You talk like a mealy-mouthed sky pilot this mornin', Doc. Death don't faze me a particle. I've spit in his eye too often for that. And I got no need to make my peace with God, never havin' had a fallin' out with Him. What I mean is—Randie."

"Leaving her with a down-grade white elephant ranch?"

Locke put on his battered Stetson, cuffed it back on his onion-bald pate. Indignation made his eyes snap.

"Broken Key ain't a white elephant, Doc. It'll come back when the rains do."

Doc grinned. He had deliberately needled Fred's temper, hinting that Broken Key was a liability rather than an asset to pass down to Randie. Not too long ago, when Randie Locke was a pig-tailed tomboy, her dad had been worth nearly a million. Not that Fred Locke ever put on airs; he was old-shoe, as unpretentious as a two-bit nester.

"It ain't debts that worry me, Doc. It's knowing my girl has taken a shine to Cloyd Weber. Leavin' her future to a shyster, a damned Pike County outlander to boot, ain't a good feelin' for a man to carry to the grave with him."

"Randie's that serious about Weber?"

"They ain't engaged, exactly, but I notice she's been thumbing through the bridal fashion pages of the mail-order catalog lately. Wasn't for her promise not to get married until she turns twenty-one, wouldn't surprise me if Weber could of talked her into an elopement."

Walking to the door with his client, Doc Ashton said inanely, "We can't control the ways of a woman's heart, Fred. Cloyd is an up-and-coming legal light. Got his sights set on occupying the attorney general's office over in Sacramento. Married to Randie, he might even go as far as Washington, D.C."

Locke grinned bleakly. "Just the same, I'd always sort of hoped she would fall in love with Tuck. There's a man who could pull Broken Key out of the red ink. For all his being

15

a slick-ear younker, Tuck Clayburn knows cattle. And he loves Broken Key as much as I do."

Locke opened the door and stepped out into the hall, facing the steep stairs leading down to the street level. He turned, offering his hand as casually as if this had been just another routine chat.

"I might point out," Doc Ashton said, hesitating in the manner of an old friend who was loath to intrude on another's personal affairs, "that Tuck Clayburn is your legally adopted son."

Their hands held their grip. "I know," Locke commented. "That's the trouble. Bein' raised together like they were, Randie feels toward Tuck like she would a brother. I doubt if she ever gives a passin' thought to marryin' him. It's somethin' a man can't discuss with his motherless daughter. If Molly was here——"

Locke was half-way down the stairs, clinging to the shiny banister bar for support, when Doc Ashton called after him, "That wasn't exactly what I meant, Fred. You're leaving Broken Key to Randie, according to that will I've been keeping in my safe for you."

Locke turned to stare up at his friend.

"I wanted to leave it fifty-fifty to her and Tuck Clayburn, but Tuck's touchy on that point. Seems to think I've done enough for him, takin' him in when he was a maverick orphan and all. Except for that one score, Tuck's my son. On the matter of a legacy, he won't touch anything he says belongs to Randie."

Ashton nodded. "I know. But it's your decision, not his. If the whole ranch went to Tuck— Give it some thought, anyway."

The two friends exchanged salutes and parted. Doc turned into his office heavy-hearted, and Fred Locke, emerging from the stair door, turned left to enter the lobby of the Cattlemen's Bank.

Another pioneer, Clement Moon, had founded this bank more than thirty years ago when, as a local merchant, he had grubstaked prospectors who were combing the deserts roundabout for the lost Gunsight and Breyfogle Lodes. In '66 one of his bewhiskered clients had made the discovery strike in Wagongap Pass from which the boom camp of Highgrade had sprung.

Moon's share of that claim had built this three-story brick building. The Highgrade boom was short-lived, but Wagonspoke was a cattle town with permanent roots. The bank was its anchor in the hard times that now paralyzed the rangeland.

Fred found Moon seated at his desk in his private office. A look of despair was in the eyes of the venerable, kindly banker, mellow at eighty, as he rose to shake hands with his oldest depositor.

"I know, Clem," Fred Locke chuckled. "You know I wouldn't be here if it wasn't to ask for an extension on my notes. But you'll grant it. You know Broken Key will prosper once this drought has broken. Maybe that will be next year—*quién sabe?*"

Clem Moon motioned the rancher into a chair, then settled his corpulent bulk behind the desk.

"Between you and me and the hitchin' post, Fred," Moon said hoarsely, "I have never listed the ninety thousand I loaned you as a potential liability on the bank's books. Broken Key is good for it. But——"

17

"But what, Clem?"

The banker drummed his desk top with nervous fingertips.

"Your notes—the third extension of them, that is—fall due in less than a month, Fred."

Locke massaged his chest, a numbness shooting through him.

"I know that. I came in to ask for another year——"

Moon's gaze met Locke's directly now, for the first time.

"Fred, I sent you a letter only this morning, telling you about this—this change of status. It'll be in your box when you get back to Broken Key this evening."

Locke came unsteadily to his feet.

"What do you mean, change of status? You're not going to foreclose, Clem? After Broken Key's deposits were the only thing that kept you solvent through two panics?"

Clem Moon's cheeks stained scarlet to the roots of his silvery mane.

"Fred, I—I overextended the bank, trying to tide you cowmen through this dry period. I—don't own the bank any more. Not since yesterday. The new owner—has retained me to run things, the same as before. But I no longer have final authority to extend or to foreclose mortgage loans."

A wild alarm coursed through the Broken Key rancher. He sat down as suddenly his knees turned rubbery.

"Who did you sell out to, Clem?"

Moon ran a finger around his buckwing collar, seeming to cringe deep inside himself.

"The letter—tried to explain. The only man with enough ready cash to assume the bank's obligations. The worst

18

enemy, I guess maybe the only enemy you got, Fred. Kyle Kruze."

The name re-echoed inside Locke's head like a gunshot in a confined canyon.

"Kyle Kruze? You sold your bank to a tinhorn gambler?"

Moon stared unhappily at his hands.

"Like I said, Kruze was the only man with money——"

Locke pressed his fingertips to his throbbing eyes. Kyle Kruze, operator of the Montalto Casino, the card-shark who had parlayed a deck of cards into the ownership of Wagonspoke's choicest real estate, the one man whose power in this town had presented a threat to the law and order Fred Locke had stood for through all the years.

Kyle Kruze, the man who still carried the scar of a bullet from Fred Locke's gun, the result of an inconclusive shoot-out in front of this very bank ten years ago. The man who, even as he writhed under the scalpel of Doc Ashton, had sworn to even accounts with the Broken Key boss if it took the rest of his natural life.

The quarrel had had a trivial genesis, growing out of a marked card in the last poker game Fred Locke had ever indulged in. But it had led to a challenge and gunplay. Kruze knew, as did the townsmen who had witnessed their duel, that Fred could have put the bullet in his heart instead of his wrist.

"Why—this means Kruze will throw me off Broken Key on July tenth, about a month from today. You realize that, Clem?"

Somehow the calamity seemed easier to face, putting it into words this way.

Moon nodded, misery in his eyes. "I'll do what I can to

19

hold Kruze off, Fred, but the final decision has got to come from him, now. This bank is being run from the back office of the Casino, not this desk."

Locke slid his chair forward, reaching for a writing tablet on the banker's desk. He snatched a penholder from a spiral rack at Moon's elbow and for the next few minutes the only sound to break the quiet was the scratching of the steel nib on paper.

When he had finished, Locke read over what he had written, blotted it, and thrust the paper across the desk to his old friend.

"Keep that in my vault box—until the proper time comes, Clem. It is my last will and testament."

Moon donned a pair of glasses and glanced over the document. Then he looked up, aghast.

"You can't do this. Bequeath a million-dollar ranch to your foreman and cut your own daughter off with a few head of cattle——"

Locke said, "Randie will understand. And Tuck Clayburn is more than my ramrod. He's my son, Clem, in all but name."

Moon pulled off his glasses and polished them nervously.

"You don't seem to understand, Fred. I think the reason Kruze bought me out was so he could be in a position to strike you where it would hurt most. A month from now you won't own an acre of land or a single head of stock."

Fred Locke nodded, coming to his feet. He felt a sublime release of tension, a feeling of having indeed put his house in order.

"I'm thinking," he said enigmatically, "that Kruze might not be so anxious to foreclose on Broken Key if he knew

Tuck Clayburn was the man he had to buck. Tuck wouldn't let the spread go without a fight."

The old banker heaved himself out of his chair.

"Damn it, Fred, you ain't makin' sense. You'd have to die in order to bring that situation about, and you've got a good twenty years left. And Tuck Clayburn couldn't accomplish the impossible, where money is concerned."

"He's young. There's plenty of land left in this country. With Randie's herd for a starter, he might——"

"What you want," Moon broke in, "is a quit-claim deed transferrin' your spread to Clayburn, then, not a bequest."

Locke's gnarled hand was on the doorknob now. There was an almost wistful note in his voice as he said, "As long as I live, Clem, I aim to fight my own battles and shoulder my own loads. But when I'm gone, I'd like to know a fighter like Tuck Clayburn is helpin' Randie buck the troubles I left behind me."

Leaving the bank, the old man headed for Gabe Garbie's Valley Mercantile Store, where he had left his spring wagon backed up against the loading platform of the feed warehouse. He had to pick up some oyster shell and bran mash for his laying hens back at the ranch.

Locke went into the deserted feed warehouse. He sized up the hundred-pound sacks of crushed shell, remembering what Doc had told him about hoisting forty-pound saddles.

He turned to look through the warehouse's archway. It had never occurred to him before, but the steeple of the church reminded him now of a finger pointing toward God. And Molly.

chapter 2

TUCK CLAYBURN blew smoke from the bore of his Colt. His ears still sang from the gunshot which had sounded like a cannon blast down in the bottom of this glacial pothole, fifteen feet below the surface of the surrounding country. But the silence which followed his shooting of the crippled steer was welcome, after the dying beast's piteous clamor.

The steer was the fourth which Clayburn had put out of misery in the last ten minutes. The other three carcasses lay half-submerged in the green-scummed water which had become stagnant weeks ago when the seep dried up.

Mosquitoes hummed around the Broken Key foreman as he studied the Rafter J brand this last steer carried. That showed to what lengths a thirst-crazed brute would go for water. This pothole was at timber line, a good fifteen miles from Frank Jessup's range.

Cows were ordinarily cautious beasts, but this Rafter J steer had found water fifteen feet below the rim of the pothole. Perhaps baited by the three bawling Broken Key steers who had already plunged over the brink, the animal had jumped.

The fall had snapped both front legs and one horn. Ironically, its threshing muzzle was inches short of the slimy pool. Clayburn could not tell, from the emaciated condition of the animal, how many days and nights it had lain crumpled here, dying slowly.

The agonized chorus of injured animals, trapped in the pit, had not reached the ears of man, for no one traveled in this remote corner of the Lavastones in the heat of summer. Clayburn had not scouted this far back since last fall; in all the years he had ridden for Fred Locke, he had not known this pothole existed. An ugly, slow-spiraling cloud of red-necked buzzards, glimpsed this morning against the brassy sky from ten miles away, had led Tuck Clayburn and Ben Tweedy to the scene.

The mercy executions were over now, and old Ben was up the slope chopping down piñon pines for posts so they could fence off the potential death trap. It might take another week or ten days for the punishing California sun to evaporate the seepage from this hole.

At that, Clayburn reflected bitterly, these animals were luckier than the scores of slat-ribbed, knobby-jointed Broken Key cattle he and Tweedy had counted, coming over from Summer Range.

All the water those animals could hope for was the dew they licked off the rocks at night. The buffalo grass was long since gone, baked brown. Only screw-bean mesquites kept the scattered herds alive, the same food which nourished the wild burros in Death Valley's burning sink.

Clayburn ejected the four spent cartridges from his .45 and slowly reloaded from his belt loops. He felt an overpowering sense of claustrophobia. He had only come down in this pothole after shooting the three Broken Key steers from the rim because the fourth victim's agonized threshings had carried it out of view under the overhanging lip and he knew he wouldn't be able to sleep nights, letting a crippled animal die of slow starvation.

The heat which had put its blight over the entire Southwest had left its stamp on the young Broken Key ramrod. There were concave shadows in his leather-browned cheeks and the skin was pulled shiny-taut over his facial bones.

Endless hours every day in saddle, checking on the condition of Fred Locke's doomed herds, patrolling a range area half as large as the state of Rhode Island, had whittled his body down to a lean, rawhide hardness. His cotton shirt sagged loosely where perspiration had not plastered it to his back and chest.

The years in saddle had put their warp in his rangy legs. Rope and branding iron had calloused his palms and the inner surfaces of his fingers. Summer suns and the glare of winter snowfields had etched tiny crowfoot wrinkles at the corners of his eyes, which were perpetually narrowed as if from squinting into far distances.

Clayburn made a final round of the seepage pond's perimeter, making sure the greening foliage concealed no cattle too weakened to bellow their pleas for a merciful bullet. Satisfied that this carnage pit had taken its last victim, Clayburn walked over to the pleated rawhide reata which hung from the north edge of the pothole, donned his fringed buckskin gauntlets for better purchase, and started climbing.

His cowboots swung inward, but the time-polished granite rock facing gave no footholds. Emerging from this hole was a hand-over-hand business, and the drag of his

24

hundred and seventy pounds put a severe tax on the muscles of his back and shoulders and forearms as he scaled the makeshift rope ladder.

Ten feet up, the sun's glare beat against him, and he hooked a chap-clad leg around the rope as a brake while he adjusted the angle of his flat-crowned beaver Stetson. A thermometer would have registered over 140 here.

Then he was hooking a spurred boot over the rim and the taut rope, dallied to the high horn of his claybank gelding's saddle, felt like a stretched wire under his gloves before he climbed out on solid ground and began reeling in the lass' rope.

This pothole was at the five-thousand-foot level where timber was scant. Half a mile away, he saw Ben knocking the limbs off his last piñon post. Anticipating what they would find in the shadow of the winging buzzards, they had brought along a coil of barbwire to fence off this deathtrap.

Clayburn buckled his coiled rope to saddle pommel and took a drink from the canvas water bag tied behind his cantle. The claybank was nibbling at a half-dead clump of bunchgrass. Everything about the California landscape was sterile, dying if not dead. It had been four years since the rocks here had glistened with rain water.

It had not always been like this. Tuck Clayburn's earliest memory of Broken Key was of an overall greenness—lush buffalo grass on the valley floors and mid-way up the Lava-stone footspurs giving way to yellow aspens and then the pines. And on the divide the snow usually held on until mid-summer.

Now the closest snow was above the twelve-thousand-foot level on the Sierras, far to the west. From where he stood,

Clayburn could see the inaccessible white patches on the flank of Mount Whitney, its eastern face sheer and bald, too steep to hold snow even when drought was not present.

To the north loomed the barren corrugations of the Cosos and the Argus Ranges; in the nearer distance, to the east, the high Furnace peaks, black with pine growth, and beyond, Telescope Peak, naked of snow for the first time in any living man's memory, standing guard over the western rampart of Death Valley's awesome, sub-sea level floor.

It had been almost a week since Tuck and his old roustabout had saddled up and left the home ranch overlooking Verde Valley to scout range conditions.

Wherever they rode, the story had been the same. Coyotes had feasted on fallen calves, leaving their skeletons to bleach in the merciless sun. The sky was aswarm with buzzards, drawn from as far away as Arizona and Old Mexico by the promise of carrion. The smell of death was everywhere, day and night.

As far back as two years ago, Fred Locke had sent his young ramrod into Nevada in search of grazing land outside the parched area, where they could salvage their herds on leased land. But everywhere the situation was the same. This drought was no localized calamity; cattle were perishing by the thousands on the other side of the Sierras, and in the usually lush pastures between the Coast Range and the Pacific Ocean.

All a man could do was wait and pray for rain—and watch his cattle die.

In all the far-flung leagues of Fred Locke's Broken Key domain, here on the Lavastone uplands, there was only one bright spot in the picture of death and bankruptcy. That was the high basin the Indians had called Lake-in-the-Sky, but which more prosaic ranchmen knew as the Summer Range.

Ordinarily, Fred Locke staged a spring cattle drive to Summer Range; he had leased a portion of it to Frank Jessup's Rafter J for as far back as Tuck could remember. Grass grew belly-high to a cow the year around there, its roots fed by underground sources of moisture.

But last year, Locke had been forced to hold that mountain-locked oasis for a tiny fraction of his own stock, the little jag of cattle, five hundred head or so, which Fred had branded R Bar L and was holding in trust for Randie when she turned twenty-one next spring.

Clayburn and Tweedy had camped last night in Summer Range basin, alongside red-rimmed Indian Lake. In normal years it covered thirty acres but this year it had been reduced to a pond one-fifth that size.

Inside this basin, however, a cattleman's Eden existed. Randie's cattle were sleek and fat. If the lake didn't dry up, surely next year would see rain clouds crossing the Sierras to restore the green mantle to this fertile land and make a cowman's lot worth living again. If it didn't, even Summer Range was doomed.

Tweedy was coming down the slope now, gnomelike in saddle, snaking a dozen fenceposts at rope's end. Tweedy had been a fixture on Broken Key long before Tuck had been orphaned as a stripling of ten, in Nevada's Amargosa Desert when a band of Indians had attacked the family wagon, California-bound from Kentucky.

A Panamint squaw, noting Clayburn's black hair and eyes and supple build, had taken him to her hogan on the

27

edge of Death Valley's salt flats, intending to raise him as an Indian. Fred Locke, scouting the country around Ballarat for wild goats, had rescued the white boy from a *rancheria* in Surprise Canyon and had adopted him as the son he had yearned for for so long.

He had been christened Gamaliel, after his father, but the Broken Key hands nicknamed him "Kentucky" and the abbreviated Tuck was the result. He had fitted into ranch life as if born to it, and had attached himself to the infant Randie as if she were his sister by blood.

Old Tweedy, riding in, glared at the posthole digger still lashed to Tuck's saddle.

"Diggin' postholes is above a foreman, hey?" the roustabout demanded surlily. "I figgered these posts would be ready to set by the time I done my tree-choppin', and all I'd have to do would be to string bob-wire while you rested."

Tuck grinned, taking no offense at what he knew was good-natured grousing on Ben's part. By rights, Ben should have held down the ramrod's post on Broken Key; instead, he had joined Fred as the kid's tutor during his growing-up years, grooming him for the responsibility he now held.

"One of Jessup's critters was down there, Ben. Where is all this going to end?"

Tweedy took out a cut plug and a wicked-looking bowie knife and started paring a replenishment for the cud he kept tucked between his toothless gums, asleep or awake.

"My j'ints ached last night. That means wet weather's comin'."

"Your bones say when rain's due?"

Tweedy squinted at the brassy sky.

"This fall. If she don't cloud up by Thanksgivin', I'm callin' for my time and goin' back to prospectin'."

Tweedy had made and lost a fortune in the Wagongap diggings during the big bonanza which had flowered and died at Highgrade in '66, and he annually threatened to return to the ghost town and find the vein he had followed to its dead-end fault. The other end of that vein was still waiting for a miner's pick to uncover it, a vein yielding ore worth $200 to the ton at the Highgrade stampmill. The mill was still there, wasn't it, waiting for another gold rush?

"I'll stick it out with Broken Key," Clayburn said, unstrapping the posthole digger from his saddle. "Even if we lose every head of stock we own, Broken Key ain't licked as long as we got that nest-egg of Randie's beef over on the Summer Range."

Tweedy snorted, watching his young boss go to work on a posthole. In this flinty ground, they would be here two days stringing wire around the pothole. But time didn't matter much this summer. They had left a pack mule and supplies for a month's camping at the water hole this morning.

"Only thing that's holdin' Broken Key above water—or above the dust, I better put it that way—is the fact that Clem Moon is a rarity among bankers, kid. Any time he chooses, Moon could take over this outfit, Locke stock an' bar'l. And don't you forget it."

Clayburn looked up from his back-breaking work.

"Don't you forget, Ben, that Clem Moon's bank would have gone under back in '73 if it hadn't been for Fred's money. Every other rancher in these parts, from Frank Jessup on down, took his money out and buried it. Clem

29

Moon isn't saving Broken Key because he's kind hearted. He knows he'll get back every penny he's loaned Fred—with interest."

Tweedy spat a brown stream into the dust. His pessimism concerning the future of this cattle country had no basis in inner conviction. Even during prosperous years, the roustabout found plenty to complain about.

"Tuck," he asked suddenly, "what do you think about the way Randie's takin' them calf-eye looks of Cloyd Weber's?"

The posthole digger clattered on the ground as Clayburn wheeled to face the old codger.

"We'll leave Randie's personal affairs out of it, Ben, the same as we do in the bunkhouse. Who she marries is no concern of mine—or yours."

Tweedy held his arms over his face in feigned alarm.

"Ringy as a rattler in dawg-days, ain't you? Let me tell you this, kid. If I was forty year younger, I'd damn' well do somethin' about that shyster lawyer hornin' in on my territory. I'd damn' quick let him know who was bull o' the herd where Randie was concerned."

Clayburn's mouth turned white at the edges. The flare in his black eyes should have warned Ben Tweedy, but the roustabout plunged on into deeper waters without reading the storm signals.

"You're in love with that gal, and who's to blame you?" Ben jeered. "You're in love with Broken Key, too, and I ask you, what would happen if Randie was Missus Cloyd Weber when old Fred kicked the bucket and the ranch was hers? You think that fancy-pants Missouri dude would stay on to run cows this far from Sacrymento's statehouse?"

30

Tuck Clayburn returned to his work with a savage zeal which convinced Ben that he had hit a bulls-eye.

"She ain't your sister, you know——"

Tuck Clayburn dropped his posthole digger for a second time. He took two quick steps toward his roustabout, fully intending to force his tormenter to swallow his tobacco cud, when a bullet spatted into the rubble at his feet and ricocheted off into space with a diminishing whine.

Tweedy bounced to his feet, leveling a trembling finger off across the heat-shimmering slope in the direction of the pine-mottled ridge where Tweedy had done his tree-chopping chores.

"We got company," the roustabout opined, "and if my eyes ain't trickin' me, he's scrooched down behind that quartz outcroppin' yander."

The spiteful crack of a Winchester's report punctuated Tweedy's drawl, and close on the heels of the gunshot another bullet plucked a dust-puff from the brim of Tuck Clayburn's Stetson.

Tweedy was scuttling for the shelter of a nearby rock, dragging his rusty old Remington single-action from his belt as he dived on his belly. When he twisted around it was to see that Tuck Clayburn was making for his ground-hitched claybank to yank his own .30–30 from the saddle scabbard.

A third slug missed Clayburn by a hair as he flung himself alongside Tweedy and levered a cartridge into the Winchester's breech.

"That quartz knob is better than a thousand yards off," Tweedy panted. "Whoever 'tis is usin' a telescope sight and I ain't the target he was after, either."

Clayburn shoved his rifle barrel over the rock, then jerked

31

it back as a steel-jacketed missile sprayed rock dust off the front of the boulder.

"Why," he demanded of the landscape at large, "would anybody want to take pot-shots at me?"

Tweedy shrugged, holstering his own short-ranged weapon as useless at this distance.

"That is a question only the gentleman up the ridge can explain to our satisfaction, reckon."

Clayburn removed his Stetson and, balanced on the balls of his feet, raised himself for another look up the slope. There was no breeze, and he could make out the faint smudge of gunpowder smoke sifting away from the quartz outcrop which Tweedy, with a vision that would have done credit to an eagle, had spotted after the first shot.

"I reckon," Tweedy continued, "I ort to be friendly-inclined toward that jasper. If'n he hadn't horned in, you'd of whupped the daylights out o' my pore old carcass for hoorawin' you about Randie. Reckon?"

The angle of the sun made it next to impossible for Tuck Clayburn to level his sights on a target, even if one had been visible. Whoever was gunning at him at such an extreme range had been uncomfortably close to his target with every shot.

Clayburn realized now that only his sudden, half-jesting lunge at Tweedy had prevented him from catching that first bullet between the shoulder blades. Standing over the posthole, he had presented a stationary target in the crosshairs of that rifle's glass. He had moved after the trigger had been pulled.

"Furthermore," Tweedy went on conversationally, hitching himself into a comfortable position against the rock, "you'd be dead now if you'd been alone here, son. Whoever that is would of ridden down here to palaver with you—and blowed you wide open when you weren't lookin'. Two of us, he dassn't risk it."

Clayburn scrubbed sweat from his forehead with his sleeve. During his thirty-one years of life, he had never been shot at before, discounting the time a drunken cowboy had emptied a six-gun at him in the schoolhouse yard at Wagonspoke over some fancied insult during a Hallowe'en square dance. The experience was not a pleasant one; it made his flesh crawl.

"But why would anybody level down on me?" he repeated. "Way out here, twenty miles from nowhere? It don't make sense."

Tweedy shrugged. "Mebbe," he said, "it was old Frank Jessup, sore because you let one of his steers fall into a Broken Key pothole. Reckon?"

Tweedy's humor was lost on Clayburn. At this moment, he got his first glimpse of the unknown gunman. A low-bent shape scuttled out of the quartz outcrop and headed for the skyline of the further ridge.

Clayburn's rifle came up and he took quick aim, allowing for the elevated position of his target before squeezing off his shot. He saw a jet of alkali pop up fifty yards short of the running man.

Before he could steady down for another try, the ambusher had vanished over the ridge, sunlight flashing off gun metal as he dipped from view.

Later, distance-muted hoofbeats reached Clayburn's ears, and a remote smudge of dust told him the rider was headed northeast, in the general direction of Verde Valley.

"I think," Clayburn said, "we'd best be getting back to the home ranch, Ben. Anybody who would be out to gun me down might have the same grudge against Fred."

They were in saddle when Clayburn spoke again. "You go back to camp and bring in the pack mule," he said. "I aim to do what I can to cut that walloper's sign and follow it in. This country's too open for him to risk holing up for another try."

Tweedy said, glancing at the hot sky, "Hope it don't rain and wash out the tracks, kid. Reckon?"

chapter 3

BEHIND the outcropping of white quartz where the ambusher had concealed himself, the naked country rock was impervious to footprints, but there were other signs which told Clayburn he had been under surveillance for a considerable period of time this morning.

Three twisted brown-paper cigarette butts told of a man's efforts to steel his nerves or steady a trigger finger for the grim business of killing a man from behind. The fact that they were lying together some five or six feet away from the four brass cartridge cases ejected by the rifle, and to the left, prompted Clayburn to wonder if the smoker had been left-handed.

"That is shavin' deduction perty fine, reckon," Ben Tweedy commented, remaining in saddle while Tuck dismounted to check the ambush site for clues. "When a man finishes a cigareet, does he allus reach for it with the same hand, or toss it the same direction?"

Hunkering down, Tuck Clayburn ran his fingers over a tiny abrasion on the quartz surface where the Winchester barrel had rested. The four shells jingled in his other hand.

They didn't tell a man much. Caliber .45–70, which would fit half of the long-range firearms in Western America.

"Whoever this hombre was," Tuck was thinking aloud when they were back in saddle, headed for the ridge over which the drygulcher had vanished, "he could have been a stranger. On the dodge, maybe, and needing a couple of extra horses."

Topping the ridge, both men hauled field glasses from cases and scanned the terrain north and eastward, picking up the faint drift of settling dust where the rider had skirted the edge of the piñons.

"He didn't need a fresh bronc, judgin' from the way them hoofs was clatterin', reckon," Tweedy observed. "I wisht you wouldn't say he was a stranger, otherwise you're inferrin' he mought just as well have laid in a shot at me instead of concentratin' on you."

Clayburn ignored the oldster's bantering, though secretly grateful for it. A man with a bullet hole in his hat brim could do with a little joshing to ease the strain.

Riding back and forth along the lower reaches of the ridge, Clayburn found the hoofprints around a dead juniper scrub which told him where the ambusher had tied his horse, out of sight from the pothole or from the slope where Tweedy had been cutting timber.

Two sets of tracks led away from the juniper. The rider had approached from the southeast, which meant he had come from the direction of the Summer Range and last night's camp. His getaway trail made a V-angle toward Verde Valley.

"We were trailed over from the water hole this mornin'," Tuck said. "He didn't just stumble across us."

36

"And whoever it was lit a shuck toward Wagonspoke, which may or may not mean anything, reckon." Tweedy leaned far from stirrup to pluck at one of the angular branches of the juniper. Tuck spurred over beside his roustabout as the old man held out his hand, thumb and forefinger pinching an object as delicately as if it were a butterfly's wing.

"The bushwhacker's hoss scratched its rump on that snag. Left some ha'r. What would you do without me, kid?"

The tiny tuft of horsehair which Tweedy had spotted had been shed by a buckskin.

"We've narrowed this down," Tuck drawled, "to a buckskin, of which we have maybe twenty in the Broken Key cavvy, and there may be a couple thousand other buckskins in Indio County. At least we won't have to worry about riders forking blacks or steeldusts or roans or sorrels. Ben, I couldn't get far without you, for a fact."

Tweedy picked up his reins. "Ungrateful whelp, talkin' disrespectful to your elders. You better git along, son, before it rains."

Tuck Clayburn lifted his claybanker into a lope, following the getaway trail of the would-be bushwhacker. He knew the futility of attempting to overtake the rider, as well as the danger of such a maneuver. What he hoped to do was keep track of the spoor and follow it to its ultimate destination. If that proved to be Wagonspoke itself, the inescapable conclusion would be that someone had ridden out to the Lavastones with the specific purpose of gunning down Broken Key's foreman.

Skirting the piñons, the fugitive's trail followed the shoul-

37

der of a lifting ridge, the crest of which gave Clayburn an unbroken vista all the way to Verde Valley and the purple loom of the Furnace Range beyond.

Fifteen miles away, on the flats of Anvil Mesa, he could see the glint of westering sunlight on the windows of buildings at Broken Key's headquarters, like diamond points through the dancing heat-haze.

Off to his right, southward, was the emerald-green basin of Summer Range, dotted with Randie Locke's grazing cattle. Old Ben was a speck on the skyline two miles away, retracing their morning ride to the Summer Range camp.

Lifting his military binoculars to his eyes, Clayburn studied the direction in which the escaping ambusher had been headed when he topped this hogback. The glasses picked up something which might or might not be the fugitive's dust trail; it was impossible to tell with the heated air pulsating off the parched earth, making the landscape shimmer as if seen through wavy glass.

Before casing the glasses, Clayburn had a look at Tweedy. The roustabout had dismounted and was walking around in circles, pointing to the ground and gesticulating mysteriously.

He saw Tweedy peering through his own binoculars. Realizing that he had the foreman's attention, Tweedy began pointing toward the Summer Range, then back toward the potholes, then at the ground.

The pantomime was clear enough to Clayburn. Tweedy was signaling him that he was still following the ambusher's tracks. That definitely established the fact that they had been trailed out from camp this morning.

This pointed to an uncomfortable possibility: the ambusher was someone Clayburn or Tweedy would recognize.

Clayburn headed on in the general northeasterly direction his attacker had taken, losing the spoor on patches of stony ground but picking it up again without wasting time riding circle.

He had no personal enemies that he knew of. The only other reason anyone might have for wanting to bushwhack him was because of his position as Fred Locke's foreman on Broken Key. And Broken Key had only one enemy who would resort to a bushwhack plot—Kyle Kruze, the Wagonspoke gambler.

Two hours' riding brought Tuck Clayburn to the wagon road which since pioneer days had served as the route from Verde Valley to the Mojave country. Covered wagon trains had laid the first ruts, following a prehistoric Indian trace; the road was maintained by Broken Key now, linking the home ranch with the town in the valley.

The road forked here, another pair of wagon tracks following a section line toward Frank Jessup's place in Escondido Valley. The tracks which Clayburn had been following from the pothole site were plainly visible in the sandy roadbed. They pointed toward the Rafter J turn-off and Wagonspoke.

Clayburn followed his attacker's trail as far as Jessup's fork, and there he saw that it was irretrievably lost. Sometime during this afternoon, Jessup, or one of his crew, had driven a jag of stock down the Wagonspoke road.

There was no point in continuing on toward town. It gave him an uncanny sensation to realize that the next time he entered Wagonspoke he might pass the time of day with whoever had triggered a long-range .45–70 at him.

Fred Locke would be interested in hearing about the abortive attempt on Tuck's life. Broken Key was only two miles away, up on the Anvil. After nearly a week away from the home spread, Clayburn was glad to be getting back.

He let the claybank take its time up the arrow-straight wagon road. Clayburn noticed by the churned up roadbed that there had been considerable traffic to and from town recently. This struck him as peculiar, for this time of year the only travel on this road, besides the pony mail rider, was when the crew headed for Wagonspoke to buck the tiger and get drunk on Saturday nights.

The sun was nearing a notch in the sawtoothed Sierra Nevadas when Clayburn topped the rim of the Anvil's flat table and saw Broken Key half a mile away.

The home Fred Locke had built for his bride was a grotesque relic of an architectural period when bay windows and turrets, iron-railed cupolas and gingerbread trimmings had been the fashion.

The ranch house was half hidden now by box elders which had been growing there when Fred had been Tuck's age. Beyond the square of lawn loomed the haybarns and cavvy corrals, neatly whitewashed, and the rock bunkhouse where Tuck had spread his blankets since his twelfth birthday, imagining himself as much a buckaroo as any puncher on Fred's payroll.

Here, where the Wagonspoke road topped the mesa wall, was a stand of cottonwoods, sere now after four years without rain. Fred had buried Molly in the little grove a few days after Randie's birth.

Tuck always doffed his Stetson whenever he rode past the

40

simple pink granite marker bearing Molly's name, with a space on it for Fred's when his time came to be laid to rest beside his mate.

Tuck was reaching for his hatbrim when he heard a horse whicker from the cottonwoods. His claybanker answered and the Broken Key ramrod reined up. He could see the glint of sundown light on the polished surface of the tombstone standing between the two largest trees. Beyond the gravesite he caught sight of an empty-saddled horse, the golden-maned palomino which was Randie's personal mount.

Tuck felt a constriction in his throat. Randie seldom visited this place, except on Memorial Day and on April tenth, the anniversary of the death of the mother she could not remember.

He reined off the road and entered the little fenced-off compound, which he had helped Fred erect to keep stray stock from grazing on sanctified ground. He was swinging from stirrups as he caught sight of the fresh wildflowers banked on the oblong mound of earth alongside Molly's grave.

Two graves!

The significance of what he saw struck Tuck Clayburn in the pit of his stomach like a physical blow. That new grave, the freshness of the flowers, meant that the man he revered as his own father had passed away during his scouting trip with Ben Tweedy.

And then he saw Randie.

The girl was kneeling on the far side of the granite monument. Day's-end light struck glints from her shoulder-long, copper-bright hair. She was not wearing her usual saddle

41

costume, man's shirt and levis and spike-heeled boots. She was dressed in mourning black.

"Randie!"

The girl came to her feet, facing her foster brother across her parent's gravestone. Her eyes, a deep blue which always reminded Tuck of a glacial lake he had seen once on a goat-hunting trip into the Panamints above Ballarat, were red-rimmed.

Tuck called her name again as he stumbled forward. Randie rounded the tombstone and walked between the two grave mounds to meet him.

Then she was in his arms, stifling her sobs against his chest, while he held her close and tried to find words to comfort her.

"We tried to bring you and Ben back," Randie finally choked out. "We sent Charlie Barcus out after you. But the second day out his pony threw a shoe and he had to come back."

Tuck pushed the girl out to arm's length, meeting the anguish in her eyes.

"Tell me, kid—was Fred ambushed?"

She shook her head, relieving him of his worst fears.

"It was a heart attack, Tuck. They found him lying in Gabe Garbie's feed store in town. It happened the same day you and Ben went out."

Six days ago. In this country, in June, burials couldn't be delayed.

"The funeral was yesterday afternoon. Tuck, I couldn't bear to think of laying Daddy away without you telling him good-bye. He looked like he was asleep, in the casket. Doc Ashton said it was instantaneous, like snuffing out a candle.

He said Dad had tried to lift a hundred pound sack of oyster shell——"

Side by side, they went to the decorated mound and knelt, without speaking, shoulders touching.

Twilight had deepened before the two led their horses back to the road, their communion over.

"If he could only have lived to see the rains come again, Tuck." Randie's voice was steady now, subdued but firm. "He was so worried, his last days—his stock dying, the ranch burning up all around him."

Tuck said gently, "It's your ranch now, Randie. You'll see the rains come and the cattle increase. Dad's grave will be green next spring. I'm sure of it."

Randie's face was a pale oval in the light of the first stars.

"It's not—my ranch, Tuck," the girl whispered." Cloyd came over from town this afternoon with the news. Dad made a new will and left it with Clem Moon only a few minutes before he died. He must have known his heart was giving out."

Tuck Clayburn froze in the act of giving Randie a hand up into the saddle.

"He didn't will Broken Key to you?"

Randie laid a hand on his shoulder, her eyes infinitely tender.

"Clem turned over the new will to Cloyd only this morning, knowing Cloyd would be handling the estate for us. Broken Key is yours, one hundred percent, dear Tuck."

Clayburn was thunderstruck. Years ago he had talked Fred out of making him a legatee to any portion of Broken Key's holdings, in spite of his legal adoption.

"Dad left me the cattle carrying my brand, the herd up

43

in Summer Range. Please, Tuck—look at me. I'm happy Dad did it that way. You deserve it—every bit as much as I."

Clayburn shook his head bewilderedly, unable to comprehend this thing. If Fred Locke had made his decision within the hour of his untimely death, it would seem as if he had known his end was near. What had been his hidden purpose?

"Tuck," Randie Locke went on, "I've got terrible news for you. I hate to tell you, so soon after finding out—about Dad."

Clayburn pulled in a deep breath.

"News?"

"Tuck—" Randie came into his arms again, knowing the shock her words would have on him. "Tuck, we stand to lose Broken Key on July tenth, when Dad's notes at the Cattlemen's Bank fall due."

"No," Clayburn said. "Moon will grant an extension, just as he would have granted it to Fred."

"Clem Moon has sold the bank, Tuck."

"Sold the bank?"

"To Kyle Kruze. Cloyd brought me that news this morning—along with the word about Dad's new will."

It was as if his world had come toppling down around his shoulders. All he could think of, in this stunned moment, was that a merciful Providence had taken Fred Locke away before the time came to turn Broken Key over to his worst enemy.

And then a following thought exploded on his consciousness like a bursting rocket. That ambush attempt at the pothole today—he believed he knew, now, the motive for that

44

mysterious attack. Kyle Kruze wanted Broken Key's new owner out of the way before he took over the spread. The ambusher he had tracked down to the valley road today had been one of Kruze's paid gunhawks.

chapter 4

Tuck Clayburn had returned from his cattle-census junket on a Friday evening. Now, at ten o'clock the following Monday morning, he and Randie sat in Cloyd Weber's law office on the upper floor of Kruze's gambling hall in Wagonspoke to hear a summation of Fred Locke's affairs.

Dr. Ashton's autopsy report had given the cause of death as angina pectoris and senile arteriosclerosis. But he had not revealed, even to Tuck and Randie, the fact that he had examined Fred an hour before his death.

The physician knew that Fred Locke had juggled those heavy sacks of oyster shell deliberately. Ashton had anticipated something like that. Life as a bedridden invalid, waiting out his few remaining months on earth, would have been intolerable to the old rancher.

Cloyd Weber laid his dossier aside and cleared his throat.

"That about sums it up," he concluded his pedantic recital of facts and figures. "Fred's last-minute decision to disinherit you, Randie, was done without consulting me, but I assure you it cannot be construed as evidence of any lack of faith in your ability to carry on Broken Key's affairs.

"We face a peculiar situation," Weber continued. "One of the finest working ranches in the State is virtually worthless as a result of the current depressed economy. The tax burden alone would frighten off potential backers outside the county. And there is the matter of $87,000 indebtedness to Moon's bank, now controlled by Mr. Kruze, who would foreclose. Tuck, you have a little under three weeks to redeem those notes."

Weber built a steeple with his white hands, a mannerism he had picked up in law school. He was younger than Tuck Clayburn by five years, a man with a rugged physique which women found attractive. Coal-black hair was roached back from his scholarly forehead in loose waves and his eyes held a sharpness which Clayburn always associated with lawyers.

Missouri-born, a man of considerable education and given to big-city ways, Cloyd Weber made no secret of the fact that he was wasting his talents in a cowtown in this forgotten corner of California.

His true opportunity awaited him in the State capitol at Sacramento. His law education had been a steppingstone to a future career in politics, and he had come to Wagonspoke four years ago on the advice of a relative who pointed out the advantage of buying out a law practice from a retiring oldster.

It was inevitable that Weber should have made Randie Locke's acquaintance. Despite his superior attitude toward the cowtown's citizenry, Weber did not let those feelings extend to his appraisal of Randie's charms.

For three years, the lawyer had pressed his courtship on Randie, and so far as Wagonspoke could tell, Randie reciprocated his affections. Fred Locke, recognizing the man's influence on a susceptible girl of more than ordinary physical attractiveness, had done what he could to forestall an impulsive betrothal. He had asked for and got Randie's pledge not to marry until her twenty-first birthday, the following April.

Beyond that, Fred Locke had done nothing to discourage Weber's attentions. But his personal dislike of the young lawyer had been no secret in Wagonspoke.

"We have three weeks to meet an obligation of nearly ninety thousand dollars." Randie broke the silence following Weber's speech. "You know that is utterly impossible, Cloyd. What it boils down to is that Kyle Kruze will move us off Broken Key the morning of July eleventh."

Cloyd Weber said gently, "Kruze is another of my clients, but it would be violating no confidence to admit that he wants Broken Key. With his other holdings in this county, it would make him the most powerful man this side of the mountains."

Randie buried her face in her hands. At twenty, she had blossomed into lovely womanhood after a tomboy adolescence in which she had learned to ride and rope and shoot along with the best of her father's crew.

Fred and Molly Locke had wanted a son, and through her girlhood, even though Fred had adopted Tuck Clayburn, she had tried to be a son to him. She had worn levis in lieu of dresses, and had ridden with the crew on every spring calf round-up and fall beef-gather since she was old enough to fork a pony. She had been wont to boast that she was a top hand on any spread; but maturity had forced full-blown femininity upon her.

48

"I am glad of one thing, in this dark hour," Cloyd Weber said unctuously. "I am glad I am on hand to shelter you from what lies ahead after Kruze takes over the ranch. This —this may not be the proper time to suggest this, darling, but I want to point out that your promise to delay your marriage until next spring has been cancelled by your father's passing. If you and I——"

Across the office, Tuck Clayburn whirled around from the street window where he had stood during the reading of Fred Locke's will. He had not wanted to come down for this necessary chore and he had consented to ride into Wagonspoke with Randie because he knew she needed him.

"Close-hobble that talk, Weber!" Clayburn snapped angrily. "This isn't the time or the place to go into your personal affairs, in front of me. The question is, how much can we salvage of Broken Key before Kruze takes over?"

Weber gave the rangy foreman a patronizing glance.

Tuck Clayburn felt the silent scorn of this fancy-pants dude from Missouri. By contrast, Tuck was all he ever pretended to be—a range-educated working cowhand without a peer when it came to cow-savvy, a man who was as skilled with gun and rope and running iron as Cloyd Weber was with his parlor etiquette and his refined vocabulary.

The day Randie had confided to her father that Weber wanted to marry her, Fred Locke had come out to the bunkhouse where Tuck was soaping a saddle to tell him how he had forestalled his daughter's plans until she was twenty-one.

Tuck was remembering now how he and Fred had swapped profanity until their ire had finally cooled off. Randie belonged on the open range with the scent of sage

49

in her nostrils and the wind and sun in her hair—they couldn't visualize her the wife of a high-falutin' lawyer with ambitions to be a congressman.

"I quite agree, and I apologize to you, Tuck," Weber said softly. "Forgive me, Randie, for allowing my personal feelings to overrule my sense of propriety."

Clayburn repeated angrily, "It goes without saying that Broken Key is lost. Any friend we could turn to is as bankrupt as we are. The thing is, we've got to salvage something before we let Kyle Kruze walk in and take over."

The lawyer shrugged.

"Aside from Fred's gun collection, which no doubt has some value, and his life insurance—a mere pittance, two thousand dollars I believe—I am afraid that the only chattel at our disposal will be the cattle bearing Randie's R Bar L brand now grazing up on your Summer Range."

Tuck Clayburn said quickly, "Tweedy and I ran a tally on Randie's stock a week ago today. It runs to five hundred and thirty head of prime stock, give or take ten. The rest of the cattle on Broken Key, counting the leased graze, runs to around three thousand head. All of it scrubby, cull stuff, and dying off at the rate of maybe fifty a day."

Weber said pointedly, "Of which every head will go to Kruze when he has the bank foreclose in settlement of his claims against the estate."

Tuck turned back to the window, wishing he had not been sucked into this interview. Somehow, with Fred's body so recently consigned to the grave, this emphasis on cleaning up his affairs tinged on the ghoulish.

He was convinced that in acting as Broken Key's attorney, Weber would in reality be working for his other client,

Kyle Kruze. Whichever way the cards fell, Weber stood to rake in a profit. But there was no other lawyer to turn to.

Tuck believed, as well, that Weber had a selfish interest in seeing Randie lose the ranch. Without Broken Key to tie her to this side of the mountains, the girl would be more willing to follow Weber to Sacramento.

Until Kruze actually became the owner of Broken Key, however, responsibility for the spread was vested in Clayburn's hands. That was what made his frustration so difficult to bear. The fight to save Broken Key from foreclosure was his fight, and it was one foredoomed to defeat.

Ninety thousand dollars seemed like all the money there was in the world. Especially to Clayburn, who had never drawn more than a range rider's forty a month and found, until a year ago when Fred had upped his salary to a hundred a month and made him his full-fledged foreman.

Through the years, Tuck had been an apt pupil for all Fred Locke could teach him. His education for his life's work had been thorough, even though it was a rough, practical one that had known little of schoolrooms.

Starting at the age of twelve, Clayburn had learned the knack of breaking a wild mustang from a master teacher. He had become adept at dabbing a loop on a *ladino* steer in the brush. He was a crack shot with six-gun or rifle. He knew how to cut a herd, read brands, doctor a sick calf on the range fifty miles from the nearest veterinary.

Now, under the impact of Cloyd Weber's unvoiced scorn, he suddenly felt acutely aware of his "crudity"—by Weber's urbane standards.

He was remembering that even if he had gotten back in time to attend the funeral service, he would not have had a

51

"Sunday outfit" to wear. Somehow, sartorial elegance had never seemed necessary to his way of life. It was a comfort, thinking over these trivial things, to realize that they had laid Fred in his casket dressed in batwing chaps, spurred boots and a sun-faded shirt.

"Tuck," Randie's voice broke into his thoughts, "I want you to sell my beef for me at the best price you can get. It will be the only way I'll have of raising the cash to meet your wages—the wages we owe the crew."

Cloyd Weber drummed his desk with a gold letter-opener.

"At the moment, I can think of but two possible markets for your herd," the lawyer said. "Your nearest neighbor over on Rafter J, Frank Jessup, might consider buying them. Or Kyle Kruze. Out of common decency, Kruze ought to meet the going market price, so he could leave the cattle where they are on Summer Range. I'll see what I can——"

Tuck turned from the window, his face bleak.

"Jessup won't buy stock when he has no range to put them on. Up to his own ears in debt to the bank, the same as Fred was. It's too early to make the drive to railhead at Bishop, with the market what it is this season."

There was a long run of silence in the office. Finally Randie Locke said hesitantly, "Then Kruze seems the only possibility?"

Clayburn crushed his Stetson in his fists.

"I'd as soon be horse whipped as to ask that money-grabbin' son——"

Randie came to her feet.

"Then I'll go downstairs and do it myself, Tuck. It's our only chance. Otherwise we will be stuck with cattle we couldn't even give away."

Tuck Clayburn walked to the door with Randie, his mood somber.

"No," he said heavily. "I won't have you going into Kruze's dive. Right now, I've got to drop in on the sheriff and tell him about what happened to Tweedy and me the other day. Then I'll see Kruze, Randie."

After Randie and her foster brother had left the office, Cloyd Weber scooped together the papers pertaining to the Broken Key estate, hastily filed them, and then made his way out into the hall.

Pausing at the top of the stairs which led down to the street, he saw Randie and Tuck stalled at the doorway by a group of sun-bonneted women who were offering their tearful condolences.

The lawyer hastened to the far end of the corridor, unlocked a door which admitted him to a private back stairwell, and hurried down to knock on the door of Kyle Kruze's office. The ground floor of this brick building housed the Montalto Casino and barroom, which at this hour was nearly empty.

Weber heard Kruze's gruff invitation to enter. He stepped quickly into the gambler's inner sanctum, his mouth compressed in a conspiratorial grin.

"Well, Kyle," Weber spoke to the man seated behind the ornate mahogany desk across the room, "I congratulate you."

Kruze turned in his swivel chair, where he had been engrossed with his accounts. The most powerful citizen in Wagonspoke, from a financial standpoint, he looked and dressed the part.

A professional gambler when he had first come from

53

Nevada fifteen years ago, Kruze had done well in this cow-town. He was a director of the Stockman's association, by virtue of his ranch holdings in the north end of Indio County. He owned a controlling interest in the flourishing freight outfit which operated between Wagonspoke and Bakersfield. Besides this gambling house, which he used as headquarters, Kruze ran a local livery and wagon yard and two saloons which he maintained to discourage outside competition in that lucrative field.

At forty, Kruze was a wealthy man. But for him greed for money and power was a driving, ruthless master, coloring his every thought and action. For years, to seize control of Fred Locke's cattle kingdom had been his prime ambition; it dated back to an abortive shooting scrape which accounted for his right wrist being deformed and bullet-scarred today.

"Congratulate me?" Kruze echoed. "For what?"

"For hitching your wagon to my star," Weber grinned. "You need the best lawyer you can get. You're lucky I hung out my shingle in Wagonspoke."

Kyle Kruze smiled faintly. A goodly part of his success he owed to Weber's legal string-pulling, and he knew it. They understood each other thoroughly; their conniving natures dovetailed in every respect.

"I'm quite aware of my good fortune in crossing your trail, Weber," he said genially. "Our alliance has been mutually profitable. Just what have you done for me now?"

Weber laughed. "It turns out you needn't have sent McCoy out to bushwhack Clayburn after all," he said, suddenly sobering. "Tuck has bowed to the inevitable,

54

thanks to my persuasive ways. I have argued him into conceding that Broken Key is lost beyond redemption."

Kruze's dark face flushed with pleasure.

"I suppose," he jibed, "you'll be doubling your fees from now on."

He came slowly to his feet, reaching out to grasp his attorney's hand. Kruze was a large man, scaling over two-twenty, and solid to the core. He wore a gambler's broadcloth coat and pleated linen shirt and sedate string tie. A three-carat diamond winked like a full moon on one finger. His coattails disguised the fact that he was never without a pair of matched Colt .45s thonged low on his flanks.

In his profession, Kruze had had to be a gun wizard. Now he was reminding himself that, since he and Weber had joined forces, the need for those guns had diminished until at this point they were practically useless ornaments. What he had formerly accomplished with brute force, Cloyd Weber's wizardry with words and manipulation of the fine points of law were doing for him, and allowing him to remain in the background as well. It was a liaison made to order for a man of Kruze's temperament.

"We will continue to work together as per our original contract," Weber said smoothly. "We are like a gun and a cartridge, Kyle—both are useless without the other."

Kyle Kruze resumed his seat, rubbing his jaw thoughtfully with his bullet-scarred wrist.

"One aspect of our association," the gambler said, "has never failed to puzzle me. You want to marry Randie Locke. If she weren't in debt to me, you would fall heir to the biggest cattle ranch in this part of California the moment she

55

became your wife. Yet you are forcing her to lose Broken Key. I don't comprehend it."

Cloyd Weber's smile widened. "It is quite simple, Kyle, if you view it from my angle. I am, at the present time, a moderately successful small-town attorney——"

"You're the best damned lawyer in California, Weber, and you know it. Don't give me that false modesty talk."

Weber went on, "I want a political career, Kyle, which is something you lose sight of. When you take over Broken Key, I will come to Randie's assistance and buy the ranch back—with funds she thinks were derived from a legacy. In reality, you will still own Broken Key——"

Kruze nodded. "It seems a rather complicated way to operate, Cloyd."

"Not at all. As the ostensible owner of Broken Key, I will be something more than a mere cowtown lawyer. I will be a landed gentleman of considerable importance in California affairs—to say nothing of having married into one of the state's most respected pioneer families. Our little arrangement will take me to Sacramento and eventually to Washington, D.C., Kyle. And I assure you I will be even more useful to you than I have been up to now."

Cloyd Weber glanced at the clock on Kruze's desk. "But I didn't come here to waste your time singing my praises," he grinned. "I wanted you to know that Tuck Clayburn will be in this morning to ask you to buy Randie's cattle up on the Summer Range. She needs cash to meet her payroll, which is almost a year in arrears, thanks to Fred's crew being the faithful fools they were."

Kruze took a Cuban cigar from his pocket, bit off the end and probed the pockets of his pants for a match.

56

"You *are* a fast worker, Cloyd. I never thought I'd see the day when Fred's foreman would pay me a visit in my own office."

Weber went on, "You will turn down Clayburn's request, of course. We hold all the aces. Jessup hasn't the graze available to accommodate Randie's stock, even if he got them as a gift. You can name your own price—and leave those cattle where they are."

Before Kruze could speak, a knock sounded on the office door.

Cloyd Weber whispered, "I imagine that's Clayburn. Don't undo my good work, now." Then he vanished into the shadowy stairwell.

"Come in," Kruze barked. The door opened and Tuck Clayburn, ducking to clear its six-foot lintel, came in.

chapter 5

Tuck Clayburn and Kyle Kruze faced each other with the detachment of men who, although they had never locked horns in the past, knew they were in opposite camps and would never be anything but enemies.

Clayburn's holsters were empty—a measure of his desperation, for he had been forced to check his guns with Kruze's barroom bouncer, Trig McCoy.

This house rule had had the enthusiastic backing of Sheriff Arnie Algar, for by dehorning his clientele, Kyle Kruze had no gun fights under his roof. The rule had been put into effect the day after Fred Locke and Kyle Kruze had shot it out following a poker-game argument.

Coming thus unheeled into Kruze's office had stung Clayburn's pride, but he knew it was the price of admission to the gambler's presence. He anticipated no trouble, but the principle of the thing hurt. It underscored his role as a supplicant; it was a tacit admission that in this situation, Kruze held the high cards, the bargaining power.

"Well, Clayburn?" the gambler said, rubbing his twisted right wrist with the fingers of his left hand. The wrist had been permanently crippled by Fred Locke's gun on that June morning more than a decade ago.

Tuck Clayburn came directly to the point, his eyes clearly showing his malice, his distaste for this chore.

"Randie Locke has around five hundred and fifty head of prime beef steers she is putting on the market. You will be taking over Broken Key three weeks from now. Buy out Randie's R Bar L stuff and we can leave the herd where it is, up on Summer Range."

Kruze blew a smoke ring at the ceiling.

"What is Randie asking for her beef?"

Clayburn consulted a slip of paper he had removed from the snakeskin band of his Stetson.

"Today's market quotation is twenty cents on premium stock like her R Bar L stuff. They'd average out a thousand pounds per head—I just got back from Summer Range over the week end."

Kruze studied the tip of his cigar. "Your price per head, then—taking your word that the cattle up there are in prime condition—is twenty dollars?"

"Twenty dollars. Randie needs some cash—all she'll inherit from Fred's lifetime of developing Broken Key. I'm putting the proposition to you on a charity basis, Kruze. Seeing that you'll be grabbing off a million-dollar spread for a white chip, you can well afford to pay ten thousand for Randie's herd."

Kruze's gold-capped teeth glinted in a slow smile.

"Twenty dollars. On a charity basis, Tuck, I'll offer five. Take it or leave it."

Tuck Clayburn's hands fisted alongside his empty holsters. The offer was a rank insult, even in an off-market year like this one.

"You can go to blazes, Kruze. I'd give the herd to Frank Jessup before——"

"No dice," Kruze cut in. "Jessup's range is crowded now. Besides which, Rafter J is in no position to accept gifts at this time or any time in the future. You understand?"

Clayburn understood. It was no secret that Clem Moon's bank had been carrying Frank Jessup, just as it had carried Fred Locke. Rafter J was another chattel Kruze had picked up when he took over the Cattlemen's Bank.

"Let's say three thousand for the R Bar L stuff grazing on Broken Key's Summer Range," Kruze went on, mockery in his voice. "As you say, it will save you and your crew the trouble of a round-up and a trail-drive when I take over Summer Range. There's no place you could drive Randie's beef anyway. Three thousand——"

Tuck Clayburn's jaws gritted as he took a tight rein on his temper. He was thankful, now, that Trig McCoy had relieved him of his six-shooter. Wildness was in his blood, which could have keyed him to extreme lengths, even to the point of drawing a gun on the gambler.

"I'll run Randie's herd over a rimrock first."

Kruze shrugged and turned back to the piles of greenbacks and coins on his desk. He reached for pencil and ledger.

"Convey my sympathies to Miss Randie," he said, "and my apologies for being absent from her father's funeral the other day. Under the circumstances, I felt my presence would have been in bad taste." He glanced over his shoulder and added, "Pick up a drink on the house as you go out, Tuck."

Clayburn turned. Hand on doorknob, he said thickly, "You had better start thinking about hiring yourself a crew to work Broken Key when you take over next month, Kruze. There ain't a Locke rider in the bunkhouse who would work for you if you paid him a hundred bucks a day."

Kruze rolled his cigar across his teeth and spoke around it.

"Better pick up two drinks on your way out, Tuck. Your nerves need settling this morning."

Clayburn turned on his heel and stalked out of the office, unable to trust his cold fury any longer. He found himself thinking, I'll shoot that mangy son of Satan between the eyes the morning he comes out to dispossess Randie.

Striding down the gloomy length of the half-deserted barroom, Tuck ignored Trig McCoy's heavy-lidded gaze as he reclaimed his twin revolvers. From their weight he knew that the Montalto house man had removed the cartridges, as a precaution following Clayburn's interview with his boss.

Fred Locke's death had not hit Clayburn any harder than this meeting with Kyle Kruze. Losing Broken Key would be like having his own two hands chopped off. He could not visualize the future, cut off from the ranch. He knew every inch of Locke's vast range, having roamed it as a boy, as a young man.

Even worse than seeing Broken Key controlled by the black-coated man who sat like a spider in that saloon office was the prospect of Randie's impending marriage to the smooth-tongued lawyer upstairs.

Tuck knew that his love for the girl he had grown up with had nothing of the fraternal in it. The love of a full-blooded man for a beautiful and desirable woman had burgeoned in Clayburn's heart too many years ago for him to know just when he had ceased to regard Randie as a sister.

Outwardly their relationship had never been otherwise. Randie loved him, Tuck knew that; but she loved him as a brother. A psychological barrier like that couldn't be hurdled. Tuck had told Fred Locke as much, the day the old man had brought him the news of Cloyd Weber's proposal of marriage.

Right now Tuck needed a drink, but he would be stirrup-drug through the jaws of perdition before he would patronize Kruze's bar. He was standing alongside McCoy's stool inside the batwings, taking his time reloading his guns, when he heard a stomp of boots on the front porch. The doors banged open to admit a towering, red-shirted oldster. Tuck recognized him as an old desert rat named Sam Scalee who sometimes wintered around Wagonspoke.

Scalee was a single-blanket jackass prospector who had more than once visited Broken Key with the idea of luring Ben Tweedy out on another hunt for the lost Breyfogle Lode. Right now, Scalee was more than a little drunk.

"Belly up to the bar, gents!" Scalee shrieked through his scrubby brush of red whiskers. "I just rode down from the gold strike at Highgrade and I'm loaded with the yaller stuff. Name yore pizen, gents—the drinks are on Sam Scalee!"

Scalee half-collided with Tuck Clayburn as he lurched toward the bar. Trig McCoy leaned from his stool to pick an ancient pepperbox pistol from the prospector's belt, and turned to hang it on the rack at his side.

"A gold strike at Highgrade?" McCoy said jokingly. "That camp's been a ghost town ever since '68, Sam. You better go sleep off your jag."

Tuck Clayburn was pushing past the drunken desert rat, heading for the door, when he saw Sam Scalee reach to his hip pockets and draw out two plump buckskin pokes.

"Dreamin' things, hey?" Scalee hiccuped. "Heft these pokes, McCoy, and don't tell me they're loaded with sand or pyrites. Highgrade," Scalee continued at the top of his lungs, "is a ghost camp no longer, boys!"

Staring after the man, Clayburn saw Scalee reel over to the bar and thump his pokes on the mahogany. The aproned barkeep was jumping to the task of setting out bottles and glasses for the customers who had joined Scalee.

Clayburn saw the bartender heft one of the pokes, heard his breathy exclamation: "Feels like the real thing, Sam. But whar'd you get this dust? Not from Wagongap Pass——"

Something kept Tuck rooted to his tracks. Through the tail of his eye he saw Kyle Kruze appear in the door of his office.

"Wisht I could take credit for makin' the strike," Scalee bragged, "but I didn't. A lousy Panamint Injun buck brung in a quill of *oro fino* to Mose Kaploon's store in Highgrade, week or ten days ago. I trails this redskin back up Shirttail crick and found a ledge that beats anything the camp worked out in '66."

Kruze had strolled over to the bar to stand beside Sam Scalee. He listened with keen interest as the desert rat continued his drunken dissertation, "News ain't been out a week, an' Highgrade is buzzin' like a bashed-in beehive. Never seed the like. Sourdoughs from the Comstock an' Hornitos an' Skidoo, a-swarmin' in by the hundreds. Never swung a pick into such float ore in my life, an' I've spent sixty year, man an' boy, prospectin' the Slates an' the Cosos an' the Furnaces. Cleaned out better'n a hundred ounces in one pocket, my first day."

The bartender shot a wink at Kyle Kruze and inquired with professional boredom, "How come you left camp, then?"

Scalee waved a drunken hand.

"Why? No likker left in Highgrade. Got me a pard holdin' down my claim up the Shirttail. Why, I paid twenty dollars for a beefsteak no thicker'n a cigareet paper day before yestiddy, an' it come from a chuckwalla at that. Thought I'd drift down to Wagonspoke an' load up with firewater an' terbaccy an' get a square meal under my belt. Then I'm headin' back for the diggin's. Yessir, boys, back to Highgrade, boomin' like a bee-tree in sage-bloomin' time. Sorry I cain't invite ye to come along."

Tuck pushed his way out of the saloon, believing nothing he had heard. Sam Scalee would be singing a different tune when he sobered up. The Furnaces had been worked out a generation ago.

He looked up and down the street, eyes squinting in the sun's glare, searching for Randie's horse. She would be waiting to learn the outcome of his business talk with Kyle Kruze.

Failing to spot her palomino at any of the racks in sight, Clayburn headed in the direction of the Cattlemen's Bank.

64

Clem Moon would be able to tell him whether or not Frank Jessup over in Escondido Valley was still in control of Rafter J, or whether Kruze had indeed seized it for unpaid debts.

Wagonspoke's main drag was in a state of high excitement. Knots of men gathered outside saloons and livery barns. Clayburn's mouth twisted with sardonic humor. This was the aftermath of Sam Scalee's entry into town, he knew. Nothing like the hint of gold to stir up excitement.

Someone bawled his name from the porch of the Valley Mercantile and Clayburn turned to see Ben Tweedy coming down the steps, carrying a shiny new pick in one hand and a shovel in the other. Tweedy had ridden in from the ranch with Randie and Tuck this morning.

"Boss," Tweedy sang out with a burred sibilance which told Clayburn the roustabout had been sucking at a bottle since his arrival in town, "you heard the big news?"

Tuck glanced down at the miner's tools Tweedy was carrying.

"You don't take any stock in Scalee's whiskey talk, do you, Ben?"

Tweedy chuckled. "Enough so I'm callin' for my time as of today, Tuck. Me, I wasn't cut out to be no cowhand anyhow. Prospectin' is my business. You know what I think? I think Scalee picked up the other end o' that vein I was workin' when the camp petered out in '67."

Clayburn said wearily, "I'm heading back to the ranch as soon as I locate Randie. You better turn those tools back to the store before you saddle up."

He left Tweedy muttering confusedly to himself, and went into the bank. He found Randie Locke inside Moon's private office, and knew by her glistening eyes that her talk with her father's banker had not been a happy one.

"Kruze offered three thousand for the R Bar L stuff." Tuck broke his news bluntly. "That's around six dollars a head for twenty-dollar beef."

Clem Moon whispered a distressed oath. "You'd better take his offer, outrageous as it is, Randie. At least it will cover your payroll deficit and leave you with a few dollars."

Randie said in a stricken monotone, "What did you tell Kruze, Tuck?"

Tuck grinned bleakly. "What I told him, Randie, doesn't bear repeating." He turned to the old banker. "Any chance Frank Jessup could——"

"No. Kruze controls Rafter J, or will as soon as the foreclosure papers can be served on Frank. That includes better than a thousand head of fair-to-middlin' Rafter J beef."

Randie Locke rose from her chair, eyes flashing.

"I'm going down to see Kruze myself," she said. "A woman can drive a better bargain in a situation like this, Tuck. I'll hold out for seven thousand—and get it."

Tuck accompanied the girl to the bank's vestibule.

"I wish you wouldn't, Randie. Let me have Kruze meet you somewhere—say over at the hotel lobby."

Randie took his hand and squeezed it.

"Afraid I'll lose my reputation if I'm seen entering the Casino? No, Tuck. This situation is too desperate to stand on pride or convention. I think I can talk Kruze into a better deal than the one he gave you."

Tuck's shoulders slumped as he saw Randie head off in the direction of the Montalto deadfall. The R Bar L herd belonged to Randie; he had no authority over what disposition she made of the Summer Range stock. Maybe she was right. Maybe a pretty woman could influence Kyle Kruze where he had failed. A girl would have public opinion behind her. That alone might cause the gambler to up his price.

He turned in at the door labeled PAUL ASHTON, M. D. and made his way up to the old medico's office. Ashton had been Fred Locke's best friend and a talk with him would be comforting.

The doctor was staring moodily out of his office window when Tuck entered. Without turning around, Ashton said, "I guess you know why Fred changed his will at the last minute, Tuck. He thought maybe you could fight for Broken Key and save the spread."

Clayburn said soberly, "A man can't win when he hasn't even got deuces back to back, Doc. I just came from Kruze's. He's enjoying his revenge."

Ashton turned slowly around. In his hands he was holding a copy of the *Wagonspoke Weekly Spectator.*

"This new strike up in the Furnaces may make things pick up around here," the medico commented. "I imagine most of your crew will head for Highgrade to try their luck, once they realize Kruze will be taking over Broken Key."

"You've heard Sam Scalee making his brag too, have you?" Clayburn asked. "Wherever Sam picked up his dust, I'll lay my last blue chip it wasn't out of the Furnace Range."

Ashton lifted a surprised glance at the Broken Key puncher.

"It isn't just whiskey talk, son. The *Spectator* wouldn't have issued this extra just now if it wasn't based on fact."

Clayburn took the newspaper from Ashton. Hand-set type loomed up at him garishly:

NEW GOLD STRIKE AT HIGHGRADE! TWO THOUSAND MINERS ALREADY ON SCENE! GHOST CAMP HUSTLING AS IN '66! SAID TO BE OF BONANZA PROPORTIONS!

The news which Sam Scalee had brought to Wagonspoke today had come from a more official source, the wires of the Reno-Bishop Overland Telegraph Company.

Tuck found himself oddly unimpressed by the gold fever already evident along Main Street. With his own world toppling, it was impossible for him to stir up any enthusiasm for anything as alien to his background as a mining boom in the Furnaces. To him, Highgrade was only a name, a mouldering ghost camp high in the hills, peopled by a scant half-dozen old timers who ran the stage station and the general store there.

He was roused out of his casual perusal of the *Spectator's* account of the Highgrade discovery by the sound of Randie Locke's voice calling excitedly from the street below:

"Doc—Doc, have you seen Tuck around anywhere?"

Tuck stepped to the window and glanced down to see the girl waving excitedly from the edge of the plank sidewalk.

"Tuck, I've got wonderful news—wonderful!"

Clayburn said dispiritedly, "I'll be right down, kid." He remarked to Ashton, "She's heard about the gold rush. Ten gets you a hundred she's hatched up some scheme to go up

68

there and pan herself a bucketful of nuggets to salvage Broken Key."

Ashton said, "I'm glad to see her smile again. Losing Fred was a tough blow——"

Randie was flying up the stairs three steps at a time before Clayburn was half-way down from Ashton's office.

Her voice held an ecstatic note as she flung her arms around his neck and kissed his cheek.

"Tuck, I got a bona fide offer from Kyle Kruze. You'd never believe it—he's going to pay me fifty dollars a head for my herd up at Summer Range—cash in advance—based on your tally! Can you believe it?"

Clayburn's head swam. Fifty dollars a head. That was two and a half times the prevailing market quotation. Ten times the offer he had made Clayburn, not half an hour ago.

"No," Clayburn said, "I can't believe it. There's a joker in the deck somewhere. Fifty dollars—that adds up to more than twenty-five thousand. Kruze wouldn't pay out that kind of *dinero* for cattle that are as good as his anyway, three weeks from now."

Randie seated herself on a stairstep, jerked off her cream-colored Stetson and ran a trembling hand through her tumbling copper hair.

"But it's true, it's true. Kruze is up in Cloyd's office right now, fixing up the bill of sale."

The girl broke off as she saw the wild light kindling in Tuck Clayburn's eyes. She saw him snap a finger, his lips moving as if he had come to some monumental decision.

"Randie," he said hoarsely, "you haven't signed anything?"

"No, of course not. I had to hurry right out and tell you——"

Clayburn sat down beside the girl, taking her hands in his.

"You're not going to sell to Kruze at any price," he said in a grinding voice. "We'll sell that herd ourselves, Randie— and for enough to save Broken Key!"

chapter 6

FOR a full minute the staircase was insulated by silence, a silence so deep that the ticking of a clock in Ashton's office overhead sounded like a beating heart. Overhead, a rafter creaked.

Tuck Clayburn's words echoed in Randie Locke's head. She couldn't have heard him right.

"Tuck—say that again!"

"You're not selling those cattle to Kruze."

"What in heaven's name has come over you? Are you crazy? We wouldn't get a better offer even if we could ship free to the packery."

Randie was staring at Tuck as if she doubted his sanity. She knew his easy-going ways, his iron self-control. He had no whiskey on his breath. She had never before seen Tuck Clayburn in such a state of excitement.

"You're not selling. We can beat his price—and for enough to settle your Dad's debts before Kruze calls in his paper. Does that make sense?"

Randie leaned back against the wall. "It does not," she admitted. "Are you sure you understood what I just told you? Kyle Kruze has offered me twenty-five thousand dollars—in cash—today! As soon as Cloyd draws up the necessary papers!"

For the first time in a long, long while—since the drought had begun its slow conflagration in the Lavastones— Randie saw boyish humor bubbling in Clayburn's eyes.

"Thank God for your impulse to bring me the news before you signed any bill of sale, Randie. Listen. Not an hour ago, Kruze let me stew in my own grease, laughing at me, offering me six dollars a head for the fattest beef stock in California. He knew he had us over a barrel and could pick up your herd at his own price, a month from now."

"I know——"

"You couldn't have even given that herd away. Nobody's got the graze to carry a measly five hundred, six hundred head. Kruze knows that as well as we do. He knew he could get your cattle for a dollar a head, three weeks from now, just by forcing us to get them off Summer Range."

Randie fanned her face with her Stetson.

"Where under the sun," she asked, "could you locate a market that would pay us almost ninety thousand dollars?"

"In Highgrade."

The girl stared at him, blue eyes uncomprehending.

"Highgrade?" she echoed. "Oh—you've been listening to that silly talk of Ben Tweedy's about another gold strike. He picked that up from some drunk this morning. He has already told me he's quitting as Broken Key's roustabout."

Tuck shook his head. "That bonanza is more than a rumor. I just saw an extra edition of the *Spectator* in Doc's office. The editor has confirmed it by telegraph. Do you know what a gold rush means, Randie? It means thousands of prospectors flooding into Highgrade. It means the price of a bed will shoot up to ten, twenty dollars a night—whatever the traffic will bear. Haven't you heard Ben Tweedy tell a thousand times how he paid twenty dollars for a helping of beefsteak in Highgrade?"

At last Randie began to understand Clayburn's excitement. She had often heard Ben Tweedy's extravagant yarns about Highgrade's fabulous heyday, when gold dust was the cheapest commodity in the camp and a hen egg had once sold at auction for fifty dollars in nuggets.

"Those miners will be hungry," Tuck went on. "Some enterprising butcher could make himself a fortune, the way food costs will skyrocket before this boom peters out. He could buy a cow and sell it down to the hoofs and horns and offal."

Randie's eyes had taken on a sparkle now.

"Then you think Kyle Kruze got the same idea——"

"I know he did. Offering you fifty dollars a head proves it. He would have the closest available beef supply tied up. He could have driven your cattle up the Pass to Highgrade and sold them for twice or three times fifty dollars. But I doubt if that was his idea, Randie. I think he wants your Summer Range herd to forestall us—in case we want to cash in on that beef market."

Clayburn came to his feet now, plans taking shape in his head faster than his tongue could express them.

"You're holding the aces now, Randie. The only other rancher in this quarter of the state with cattle to sell is Frank Jessup, and you know the condition his Rafter J stuff is in this summer."

They were heading down the stairs now. At the door to the street, Randie whispered excitedly, "What excuse will I give Kruze and Cloyd about signing those papers?"

"Don't give 'em any excuse. You ride back to the ranch and take Ben Tweedy with you. No—he's drunk. You have Spud gather the crew and head for Summer Range, right away—tonight. Have them start gathering every critter that wears your brand and earmarks. I've got to make sure we have a market waiting for us in Highgrade. I figger Gabe Garbie can supply that."

They pushed through the doorway into the punishing heat of the mid-day sun. Randie touched Tuck's arm, her eyes mirroring a torment of emotion too great for expression.

"If only Dad——"

"I know, kid."

The girl got herself under control with an effort. "You aim to drive my herd to the diggings—or sell them to Garbie here in town?"

"It's Highgrade where those cattle will be in demand, not here. From Summer Range to the summit of Wagongap Pass is a hundred miles by the South Fork of the Anviliron, maybe less by the North Fork, but the grass won't be as good on that side. That's why we haven't a moment to waste, Randie."

The girl made rapid mental calculations.

"Say a week to make the round-up, ten days for the drive—"

Tuck said, not having had time to figure up the odds himself, "We could beat Kruze's deadline with a little time to spare."

He turned away, and then, remembering something, he said in a cautious undertone, "Keep this thing strictly under your John B., Randie. Don't even tell the crew what's in the wind. If Kruze guesses what we're up to, he might try to stall us—with paid guns. This is a big thing."

Randie crossed her heart with a fingertip.

"It's the biggest gamble we'll ever make in our lifetimes, Tuck. Mum's the word, then. And luck with Gabe Garbie."

Clayburn had difficulty keeping his face austere as he headed past the bank toward the Valley Mercantile. As he was walking up the ramp, he saw Randie leading her palomino stallion from the alley next to the bank.

The Valley Mercantile was the second largest business establishment of its kind in Wagonspoke and the only major enterprise which was still operating independently of Kyle Kruze's influence. It was owned by Gabriel Garbie, a hard-fisted Connecticut Yankee who had drifted into Verde Valley in '52 after an unsuccessful stab at mining in the Mother Lode country.

He had remained here to make a fortune with a general mercantile store, had represented Indio County in the state legislature, and at the present time, as Mayor of Wagonspoke, was the only stumbling block to Kyle Kruze's total domination of the cowtown's affairs.

Making his way into the cluttered store, Clayburn found Garbie's clerks doing a brisk trade in shovels and washpans and other gear. Men Tuck had known for fifteen years stared at him without speaking, completely absorbed in their personal plans. The town blacksmith was here, abandoning his forge for the promise of treasure waiting in the mountains.

75

Housewives were here, the gold lust fevering their cheeks; cowpunchers and bartenders, two of Clem Moon's bank tellers, a hostler from the livery stable crowded the counter. All segments of Wagonspoke society were answering Highgrade's clarion call. By dark tonight, half of the town's business houses and private homes would be deserted. If this new boom ran true to form, nine out of ten of these hopefuls would have a summer's back-breaking labor for nothing.

At the rear of the store Clayburn found his old friend Gabe Garbie in his office cubicle, serenely indifferent to the bustle in his store.

Last Thursday, old Garbie had closed his trading post in honor of Fred Locke's memory and, infirm with arthritis though he was, had made the ten-mile trip out to Broken Key for the funeral.

This was the first time these two had met since Locke's death. Tuck saw the old man's eyes cloud as he cuffed back his celluloid eyeshade and sought to make an adequate greeting.

"Gabe," the Broken Key ramrod plunged directly down to business, "you're still running your branch store up at Highgrade, aren't you?"

Garbie nodded, twisting his disease-stiffened body around in his wheelchair to face Clayburn. He had been confined to a wheelchair for as long as Tuck could remember, but the ravages of his illness had not dulled his trader's acumen.

"It's still there," he grinned, "just to keep old Mose Kaploon occupied. I've lost money on it ever since the diggings petered out in '68. Looks like now I'll be doin' more business in Highgrade than I will be in Wagonspoke."

76

Closing the door on the hum of trading, Clayburn grinned, "This town will be empty by tomorrow, by the looks of it. Same thing probably going on over at Kruze's store."

Garbie folded his knobby, misshapen hands over his paunch and cocked his head.

"You ain't mentioned our mutual loss, so you got somethin' you're workin' up to. I'm finishin' inventory, son, so whatever it is, speak your piece and vamoose."

Tuck sat down on the edge of Garbie's cluttered desk.

"You've got the only butcher shop in Highgrade, Gabe. And I'll lay you odds right now that Mose hasn't got a side of bacon or a pig's foot in his barrel."

Garbie dipped his jaw, which was as close as he could come to nodding his head.

"You're leadin' up to something," the trader grinned.

"The biggest deal you've listened to since you left Connecticut, Gabe. Look. Randie's legacy from Fred was five hundred odd head of prime steers getting fat up on our Summer Range."

Garbie's face went grave. "I know," he whispered. "The grapevine has told me about Kruze fixing to take over Broken Key. It is a damned shame."

"It won't have to happen," Clayburn said. "Gabe, I'm acting as Randie's agent in offering that herd for sale— delivered at Highgrade inside of two weeks. Get the drift?"

Gabriel Garbie was a trader born and bred. His agile mind was leaping ahead of Clayburn's words.

"What," he asked tentatively, "are you askin' for those cows, delivered on the hoof? Assuming I could pasture 'em."

77

Garbie was talking like a shrewd trader, hedging, pointing up possible obstacles even at this formative stage of the deal, but he could not conceal the flush of excitement which reddened his face. He was trying to grasp what it would mean in cold dollars and cents to have a corner on prime beef in a boom town where hungry men would pay anything for fresh meat.

"There's grass and water up there," Tuck Clayburn said. "I scouted the Wagongap Pass area last summer. Not enough graze to handle a fraction of Broken Key's stock, but enough to carry over Randie's little jag for the short time before they'll be slaughtered."

Garbie tapped his teeth with a pencil.

"How much," he repeated cagily, "are you askin'?"

Tuck did some mental calculating. His monumental idea of a cattle drive to Highgrade was still so new in his own mind that he had not gotten around to any dickering.

"I'll lay my cards on the table, Gabe," he said earnestly. "You know that Kruze bought out Moon's bank. That gives him control over Broken Key. Fred's debts, spread over the past five years, tally up to eighty-seven thousand dollars."

Garbie whistled. He made a clucking sound with his tongue.

"Had no idea he was in that deep."

Tuck went on, "Gabe, your guarantee of a hundred and eighty dollars a head would net Broken Key ninety thousand. We've got over two weeks to copper Kruze's bets. Barring stampedes or other trouble on the trail up there, we can make it with time to spare. I'll have my round-up started by daylight tomorrow."

Garbie's mouth twisted in a wry grin as he repeated, "One-eighty. With today's market at twenty dollars."

Tuck, mistaking the old trader's reaction, said quickly, "I know that sounds steep. It's a price no cow ever fetched in the history of the country, I guess. But think how many steaks Mose could carve out of one steer. Old Sam Scalee told me only this morning he paid twenty dollars for a beef-steak up at Highgrade."

The old Yankee said gently, "I didn't object to your price, son. I wouldn't drive a hard bargain with old Fred's boy."

Tuck Clayburn thought, this is too good to be true. Aloud, he went on, "You wouldn't be running any risk. You were a miner yourself. You should remember how fan-tastic——"

Garbie lifted a hand to wave Clayburn into silence.

"How well I remember! I built my store in Highgrade when it was still a tent city, remember? And over on the Mother Lode, at Columbia and Murphy's and Sonora, I remember well paying five bucks' worth of dust for a fried egg and a dollar for a cup of watered-down chicory that passed for coffee. And fresh beefsteaks? They couldn't be had for any money. Not up in Highgrade in '66."

Garbie wheeled his chair around and pawed through his desk to pick up a yellow flimsy bearing the Overland Telegraph insigne.

"I just got word from Kaploon this morning," the trader said. "Guess I was among the first to know about the new strike up there. Mose says Highgrade is crowded to over-flowing already," Garbie quoted from the telegram. "Men pouring in at the rate of a thousand a week, he thinks.

79

Mose is clawin' his hair out, wanting me to get him a few wagonloads of picks and shovels and tallow candles and overalls and such-like up to him."

"He doesn't mention supplies for his butchershop?"

"Mose wouldn't, knowing the condition this drought has left our valley cattlemen in. Outside of Randie's herd, the only cows in Indio County are hide and bones, not worth renderin' for tallow. I understand Frank Jessup's thinking seriously of butchering just for what the hides will bring from the tannery at San Pedro."

Old Gabe turned back to Kaploon's telegram and went on, "Mose thinks the new boom will fizzle out, but judging from the strikes already made up there, he figgers we're safe on gambling that it will last over the winter. If Kaploon says Highgrade is back on the map to stay even for three months, I'd be a fool not to grab this corner on beef."

A vast relief went through Tuck Clayburn. He had worried about Highgrade's new bonanza turning into a flash in the pan.

"It's a deal, then?"

Garbie did not accept Clayburn's extended hand.

"Not so fast, son. It's a deal, yes—on one condition. I'll have to operate on a first-come, first-served basis."

Clayburn scowled. "What do you mean?"

"I'll buy Randie's herd, and gladly—if it reaches Highgrade before anyone else's beef. That could happen, you know. Other ranchers, say from Nevada, might get this same bee in their bonnet. On a deal running into five figures, I've got to be practical. I'll instruct Kaploon to buy the first beef he sees."

They shook hands on that proposition, a supreme confidence restoring Clayburn's good humor. He had no competition to worry about. Garbie was just plugging up all conceivable loopholes.

"I'll be too busy to drop in for another confab, Gabe. But ninety thousand dollars is a whale of a lot of *dinero*. I realize your financial situation may be shaky, the way you give credit to every saddle bum and prospector who hits you for a grubstake. I was just wondering——"

Garbie said, "I'm solvent."

"Randie will have to have cash on the barrel head when Kruze tells Clem Moon to pick up Fred's notes on the tenth of July. What I'm driving at, Gabe, is that we can't wait for you to make your retail profit on that meat."

Garbie said, "You will get your cash, subject to the proviso I just mentioned—delivery of your herd ahead of anyone else. And I'll go you one better, son, out of respect for Fred's memory and the fact that Fred on more than one occasion loaned me money, interest free, when times were hard in the past."

"What's that?"

"I'll pay you two hundred dollars a head even, delivered at my bedground in Wagongap Pass. That'll take care of the inevitable trail losses you'll have."

Clayburn's head spun. Garbie's generosity was overwhelming. All he had to worry about now was delivering the herd to Highgrade within the narrow time limit allotted him.

"One more thing before you go, son," Garbie said. "You know how much Kruze wants Broken Key. He will stop at nothing to prevent you from reaching Highgrade with Randie's beef."

81

"We're keeping the drive secret. Kruze won't know what's in the wind until he sees the herd crossing Verde on its way to the mountains."

Garbie's eyes were grave. "All right, so Kruze will get wise to the fact that Broken Key, which he believes bankrupt, has the potential gold on the hoof to redeem Locke's indebtedness. You understand the risks you'll be facing, don't you?"

Clayburn's jaw set grimly.

"I do, of course. Fred left me one priceless asset for an emergency like this, Gabe—the absolute loyalty of my crew, the men who stand to shed their blood for Broken Key's future if Kruze decides to fight."

Garbie whispered, "Your own blood would flow first of all, son. May the good Lord forgive me if I am touching off a range war, OK'ing this deal."

Tuck Clayburn left the Valley Mercantile and was heading for his horse at the courthouse hitchrack when someone called his name from across the street. He turned to see Cloyd Weber hurrying toward him.

In stony silence, Clayburn waited for Weber to speak.

"Doc Ashton tells me Randie has left for Broken Key already, Tuck. Is that right?"

"Yes. Her business was finished here in town."

Weber made a wild gesture, drawing a set of papers from his frock coat.

"Good lord, Tuck—she didn't put her signature on these bill of sale papers for the Summer Range herd. Twenty-five thousand in cash, and she lights out for home!"

Clayburn forced a laugh. "Oh, Kruze's offer to buy her herd at fifty bucks a head? She told me about that. I told her Kruze was having a little joke at her expense."

82

Weber's jaw dropped. "You—what? Tuck, you idiot—Kruze was on the level! I have his signature on these papers! All we need is Randie's signature and Kruze will hand me his draft for twenty-five thousand dollars! Does that sound like a joke?"

Clayburn appeared to be non-plused.

"I'll be hornswoggled," he said. "Tell you what, Weber. I'll take those papers out to the ranch myself."

Weber hesitated. "When will I get them back?"

"I'll send one of the boys in with 'em."

The lawyer surrendered the papers with obvious reluctance. Clayburn folded and pocketed them, undecided whether to burn them on the ride back to Broken Key or to show them to Randie tonight as proof of Kruze's desperate attempt to circumvent their new plan of action.

He found Ben Tweedy waiting for him at the hitchrack in front of the courthouse. The oldster had lashed his new pick and shovel behind the cantle of his pony's saddle.

"Just waitin' to say good-bye an' good luck," Tweedy announced. "Couldn't leave without a handshake, reckon. Wish me luck up at my old stampin' grounds, kid."

For answer, Clayburn picked up the roustabout, carried him to the brimming watertrough, and dunked him thoroughly. Tweedy, sputtering and now half-sober, choked out as soon as Clayburn put him on his feet, "Tuck, one o' these days you're goin' too fur. Why'd you douse me this-away, damn you?"

"You're riding back to the spread with me, Ben," the Broken Key boss said quietly. "During the next couple of weeks I'm going to need every rider I can lay hands on—even a broken-down old mossback like you."

chapter 7

EARLY the following morning, Randie Locke rode out to the Summer Range accompanying her father's veteran cook, Flapjack Farley, and his chuckwagon.

Even with the sun but two hours high, the high benches of the Lavastones baked in the heat. The air was heavy with the stench of rotting cattle and wherever the girl looked she saw vultures gorging on carcasses, too surfeited with carrion to take wing as the wagon rattled past.

Yesterday, this ghoulish evidence of the drought's killing breath would have dispirited Randie. But this morning, new hope buoyed her. She was realist enough to know that Tuck Clayburn's sensational plan for a cattle-drive to Highgrade and a fabulously rich beef market would not bring salvation to Broken Key without day and night sacrifice on the part of her crew.

A thousand things could go wrong on a hundred-mile trail drive at this time of year. Time was against them, unless everything worked smoothly. But Fred's dauntless optimism was grained into his daughter. Tuck Clayburn had given Broken Key a fighting chance. She could not ask for more.

Acting as Tuck's messenger, Randie had sent the crew out yesterday afternoon. Shortly before sundown Clayburn had stopped at the ranch to change horses and tell her about his deal with Gabe Garbie. Then, without stopping to eat, he had headed for Summer Range. He had left behind the papers which Kyle Kruze and Cloyd Weber had drawn up for the sale of her herd. Randie had consigned them to the cookstove.

Topping the scab-rock littered ridge overlooking the lush green floor and side draws of the Summer Range basin, Randie saw the progress which Tuck and his crew had already made on the round-up. As far as her eye could see the dust clouds were boiling from the innumerable side draws. There her R Bar L-branded steers and feeders and yearlings customarily took refuge during the heat of the day, coming down to Indian Lake for water at dusk, like deer.

Those dust clouds marked the activity of Tuck and his riders, chousing R Bar L stuff out of the chaparral. Already, the beginnings of the trail herd were taking shape on the holding ground by the water hole, which in the last few snowless winters had shrunk so that it could not be called a lake. The bawling of the sleek steers reached her ears.

Somewhere down there, Tuck Clayburn was busy with rope and peg pony, along with his men. He had allotted six days to clean up this off-season round-up; on the seventh day he wanted to be on the trail to Highgrade.

Nowhere else on Broken Key's sprawling sun-blighted range were the cattle as fat and frisky as on this high basin.

Fred Locke, years before his daughter's birth, had foreseen the coming of dry cycles and had added Indian Lake and its surrounding graze to his holdings. The rest of his spread might turn to desert, as it had this year, but his Summer Range could hold its own against drought conditions.

"Round-up's comin' along tol'able good," Flapjack called as he pulled up his chuckwagon alongside Randie's palomino to give his mules a breather. "You're lucky you got a man like Tuck to carry on for you, ma'am."

Randie's eyes softened as she turned to the range cook who had been on Fred Locke's payroll for more than thirty years. Like everyone on Broken Key's crew, from Tuck down to roustabout Ben Tweedy, Flapjack had not received a penny's pay in over two years. Yet not one waddy had quit to try his luck elsewhere.

"I know that, Flappie," she murmured. "They don't come any finer than my brother."

Old Flapjack picked up his lines. Something was obviously on the old codger's mind. He spat a gobbet of tobacco juice into the dust and said, "Now comparin' Tuck to this fancy-pants Cloyd Weber jasper who's aimin' to hitch up with you——"

"Flappie, now!" Randie warned the cook good-humoredly. "I haven't told Mr. Weber I'd marry him."

"He's shore pressin' his suit, as the sayin' goes."

She said archly, "Mr. Weber is a fine man. Half of the girls in Verde Valley would like to dab their loop on him."

Flapjack Farley snorted. "Let 'em. You wouldn't have the inside track with that shyster if——"

"Don't call him a shyster, Flappie. Mr. Weber's integrity is beyond reproach."

Flapjack grumbled profanely as he kicked off his brake and jogged the mules into motion with a handful of persuaders from his pebble box.

"Just the same, I don't cotton to a feller who plays both ends ag'in the middle. Kyle Kruze is aimin' to take over Broken Key, ain't he? And Weber is Kruze's lawyer."

Spurring the palomino into a trot as the chuckwagon began bouncing down the grade into Summer Range, Randie called back angrily, "He is also my lawyer, Flappie, and don't you forget it. Whether his other client takes over the ranch isn't in Mr. Weber's power to control."

Flapjack took refuge behind his shaggy beard as he watched the girl swing into a long lope, going on ahead.

"Danged blind fool, that's what she is," the cook snarled. "Can't she see Tuck's been eatin' his heart out for her? And she calls him brother. Hell's afar!"

Randie put her palomino on picket with the rest of the Broken Key cavvy. When Farley's wagon arrived, she set about helping the cook set up camp under the scrub live-oaks where a thousand years before Indian squaws had harvested acorns and left their midden dumps to mark this spot.

At noon the crew began drifting in, driving small jags of cattle ahead of them. Tuck Clayburn was the last to arrive, adding another dozen-odd steers to the swelling herd.

He off-saddled and walked out to the lakeside where Ben Tweedy was scrubbing the morning's accumulation of dust out of his ears and eyes. The old man was in his usual vitriolic temper, his face as red as the roundabout mud flats.

"Camp's got a grubliner already," Tweedy complained.

Clayburn felt a sharp stab of alarm. This round-up was supposed to be a strict secret. He had already begun to worry about the dust clouds they were kicking up. To anyone spotting it from Verde Valley, such a concentration of dust could mean only one thing—a large-scale beef gather.

Hearing that a rider had come out to join them at noon chow made Clayburn uneasy. He didn't want any spies snooping around. It was inevitable that Kyle Kruze would learn that Broken Key was moving Randie's herd, and might guess their destination, but he had hoped to be well on the trail before that happened.

"Who is it? Frank Jessup?"

Tweedy snorted angrily. "Fancy-pants himself."

"Cloyd Weber?" Even as he spoke the name, Tuck Clayburn recognized the leggy steeldust stallion which the Wagonspoke lawyer always rented for making trips out to the ranch.

Clayburn passed Tweedy and headed at a fast clip toward the cookfire.

Yesterday, volunteering to carry Kruze's bill of sale out to Broken Key for Randie's signature, he had led Weber to believe that someone would return the documents to town today. The lawyer was only tracking down business in coming out there. But Clayburn hadn't counted on Weber heading for Summer Range if he found the home ranch deserted.

He found Weber sitting in the shade of the chuckwagon tarp, eating out of a tin plate, with Randie seated on a packing box at his side.

As Clayburn strode up, he nodded to the lawyer and his

eyes caught Randie's, giving her a tacit warning. She had given him her word not to divulge the reason for this Summer Range beef-gather. Above all, he wanted to keep their secret away from this lawyer who was on Kyle Kruze's payroll.

"Randie just told me she has turned down Kruze's offer to buy this herd," Weber said, meeting Clayburn's noncommittal stare. "I presume that is your doing, Tuck. I cannot help but feel you are making a mistake."

Clayburn said, having difficulty keeping his ill-will toward Weber out of his voice, "I told Kruze yesterday I'd drive these steers over a rimrock before I'd sell them to him."

Weber eyed the Broken Key foreman over his coffee cup.

"Twenty-five thousand dollars is a high price to pay for venting your spleen on a man you don't like, Tuck. Especially when the money isn't coming out of your pocket."

Clayburn heeled away and went over to the wagon to get his eating tools. Flapjack Farley was ladling soup for him when Randie came up beside him.

"Cloyd is very curious to know why we're out here rounding up my cattle," she whispered anxiously. "What can I tell him?"

Clayburn shrugged. "Let him think we're selling to Jessup. Or that we're gambling on a drive to Bishop. Weber doesn't have enough cow-savvy to think this thing through."

Randie said heavily, "He's not quite that stupid, Tuck."

Heading back toward the shade of the tarp where Weber was lighting an after-dinner cigar, Clayburn said, "As long as your friend Weber is working for Kruze, we've got to consider him an enemy in the camp. Stall him off."

Clayburn took a seat on the wagon tongue, pointedly avoiding going to join Weber. He saw Randie and the lawyer wander off in the direction of the remuda.

Randie tried hard to make her voice sound convincing as she said, "This round-up is Tuck's idea, Cloyd. He distrusts Mr. Kruze's offer. And so do I."

The lawyer reached down to break a stem off a sage bush and began nibbling it. His eyes ranged off beyond the camp to where three of Clayburn's punchers were riding circle on the grazing herd across the waterhole, keeping them bunched.

"Randie," Weber said heavily, drawing in a deep breath, "I thought you might be interested in knowing that I am no longer Kyle Kruze's legal representative."

The girl turned on him in astonishment.

"Cloyd! You mean you and Kruze have had a quarrel?"

Weber took the cigar from his teeth and said gravely, "No. I returned his retainer and told him I could no longer consider him a client of mine—until after the Broken Key estate had been settled, at any rate."

Randie Locke felt a glow of pride suffuse her cheeks.

"Cloyd—why? Mr. Kruze's business must be considerable—he must have been your best-paying client."

Weber looked at the ground.

"He was. But I could not fight my conscience, Randie. You are my client also, and so is Tuck Clayburn, although I realize he dislikes me and always has. I couldn't, with honor, represent your interest and Kruze's also, when they are so diametrically opposed."

90

Randie reached out to touch Weber's hand. She had never felt warmer toward this outsider than she did in this moment. He was not a Westerner and never would be; by temperament and upbringing he was not equipped for frontier life. Yet she knew the price, both moral and financial, Cloyd Weber had paid when he cut himself away from a lucrative source of business such as Kyle Kruze and his many enterprises represented for a lawyer.

"Why did you do it, Cloyd?"

He turned his head to look down at her, his dark eyes warm with emotion.

"Turn my back on Kyle Kruze? Because I love you, Randie. And because I could have no part in helping Kruze rob you of this ranch you love."

Randie put a hand to her throat, rubbing the sudden ache there.

"Cloyd, you make me very happy."

The lawyer turned to face her, reaching out impulsively as if to take her in his arms. She glanced toward the cow camp and shrank away.

"Cloyd—please—not in front of the boys."

He said in a gusty undertone, "Randie darling—I may be leaving for Sacramento in a day or two—to take up some legal matters with the state attorney general. I expect to have a wire confirming my appointment with him when I get back to town today. What's to prevent you from coming with me? We could get married before we leave and sort of make a honeymoon of it. San Francisco——"

Randie Locke said heavily, "You know why I can't marry you this year, Cloyd."

Impatience needled the man. "But your father's death—

91

you are no longer bound by that nonsense about waiting until you are twenty-one, Randie. Next April is so far away."

She looked at him, her eyes pleading for understanding.

"Please, Cloyd, don't ask me to break my promise to Dad so soon after his going. Please——"

She turned, heading back to the camp where Clayburn and his riders, their brief noon rest at an end, were beginning to saddle up for a new stint of brush-popping.

Catching up with her, Cloyd Weber said in an offended tone, "Why the rush, Randie? What's this round-up all about, anyway? Where is Clayburn moving these cattle?"

Randie came to a halt. "I'm sorry, Cloyd. I can't tell you what Clayburn's plans are. Everything is so mixed up— please don't think I'm churlish. And good luck on the Sacramento trip. How long will you be away?"

The lawyer shrugged. "I may not even go. It depends on whether I can get an appointment with the attorney general. If I do go, it'll be for a week, not longer."

"Come out to Broken Key as soon as you get back, then."

She was dismissing him. Annoyance rankled Weber, annoyance and the beginning of a conviction that he was ₁osing Randie's love.

He saddled up and his thoughts on the return ride to Wagonspoke were concerned with something he had overlooked at the time—Randie's mysterious refusal to explain the reason for the Summer Range round-up.

Something important was in the air, something mysterious. Tuck Clayburn was up to something—but what?

He reached town at the end of the day and went directly

to the Overland Telegraph office on the off chance that he might have had a reply to certain messages he had dispatched to the state capital during the week.

The telegraph operator was not at his instrument desk. The sounder was clattering busily, but the dots and dashes made no sense to Weber.

Knowing the telegrapher's habit of spending more time drinking beer than he did on duty, Weber made his way behind the counter and began shuffling through a basket full of tissue paper flimsies, carbon copies of messages transmitted and received during the day. The lawyer knew he was trespassing, that going through these papers was as serious an offense as rifling the U. S. Mails, but damn it all, he told himself, it was the telegrapher's responsibility to stay on duty.

He was leafing through the flimsies, hoping to find a message addressed to himself from Sacramento, when his eye was arrested by the name "Broken Key" on a message.

Picking it up, Weber's eyes raced over the scrawled writing, realizing that he had stumbled across something vitally important. The message was addressed to Mose Kaploon, the general merchant up at the gold camp, and bore the signature of Gabe Garbie of Wagonspoke:

HAVE CONTRACTED WITH BROKEN KEY FOR FIVE HUNDRED HEAD BEEF CATTLE DELIVERY DATE APPROXIMATELY JULY TEN. MAKE CERTAIN WILD-ROSE FLATS AVAILABLE AS HOLDING GROUND.

Restoring Garbie's confidential message to the Overland Telegraph basket, Weber had only a fleeting interest in the

93

object of his original search—a brief wire from the attorney general's office regretting that he could not grant Weber's request for an appointment on the date desired, owing to pressure of state business.

His planned trip to Sacramento was unimportant now.

Leaving the telegraph office without catching sight of its truant operator, Weber headed toward Kyle Kruze's Montalto.

"So that's why Randie was so secretive about that round-up at Summer Range," he muttered, a wild excitement in him. "Kruze will be very much interested in hearing about Garbie's deal——"

chapter 8

AT sundown of the third day of the Summer Range beef-gather, Tuck Clayburn rode in from the bed-ground across the lake to join his saddle-weary crew at Farley's chuckwagon. He was in high good spirits, despite sixteen hours in the saddle.

"Tally shows four hundred and twelve head choused out of the draws, all prime stuff," the Broken Key foreman sang out as he off-saddled. "With any kind of luck we'll finish this round-up tomorrow noon, boys. Three days ahead of schedule."

Spud O'Rourke, the cavvy wrangler, dumped his dishes in the wreckpan and came over to where Tuck was ladling mulligan stew out of Farley's black pot.

"Tuck, this is damned hard work for summertime, and us not knowing what's back of this round-up," the wrangler began. O'Rourke had practically grown up on Broken Key along with the ramrod, and he was not a man to hold his tongue with the boss. "And now the rumor's out that you've given orders we got to stick around camp tomorrow night instead of lightin' over to town for a nip of red-eye and a fling at buckin' the tiger."

Clayburn seated himself Turk-fashion at the outer edge of the cook-fire's light and grinned around at the circle of work-weary faces. The hard pace had tired these boys to the bone and even the cheeriest of them were beginning to crack under the strain.

"That's right, boss," spoke up Flapjack Farley, assuming a cook's prerogative to act as spokesman for the men. "You been actin' all-fired mysterious about this whole deal, and so did Randie before she went back to the ranch yesterday. You got to let the boys have a chance to play curly wolf just like old Fred used to do."

Clayburn said quietly, "Trips to town are out, boys. I reckon the time has come, though, to let you in on this deal. I've kept it under wraps up to now because the fate of Broken Key depends on keeping word of this round-up quiet."

Lanky Charlie Barcus, at seventeen the youngest member of the crew, spoke up from across the campfire:

"By Gawd, boss, I got a date with a gal for that dance over at the schoolhouse tomorrow night and I aim to be there."

Clayburn came slowly to his feet, sensing the first faint stirrings of mutiny among his men.

"You won't want to go to that dance, Chuck, when I tell you why I want no Broken Key men drifting around town getting drunk and talking out of turn."

Barcus said huffily, "I'm listenin', boss, but I ain't sayin' I'll like it."

Clayburn's lean face was etched with harsh ruts of fatigue as he looked at the questioning faces of his Broken Key crew.

"You all know Kyle Kruze has taken over the bank in town," he began. "July tenth is the date Fred Locke's notes fall due—for the third successive year—at Clem Moon's bank. If we don't raise around ninety thousand dollars by that date, you'll be working for Kyle Kruze, not me. This you already know."

The men stirred uneasily, reluctant to meet the ramrod's eye.

"I've got a buyer for Miss Locke's steers," Clayburn went on. "Gabe Garbie is paying two hundred bucks a head for every steer we rustle off of Summer Range. Payable when we get the herd up to Garbie's place at Highgrade."

A long run of silence followed Clayburn's momentous announcement. Each man in the ragged circle was sizing up its implications in his own manner.

"If Kyle Kruze gets wind of what we're doing here," Clayburn went on, "we'll find ourselves bucking his gunslammers. Kruze wants Broken Key and he'll go to any lengths to keep us from bailing out Fred's debts."

Clayburn resumed his seat and picked up his grub plate.

"That is why," he said, staring across the dying fire at Charlie Barcus, "I can't have you traipsing off to the dance in town tomorrow night, Chuck, and maybe getting drunk to the eyebrows and bragging about this trail drive we've got coming up."

A subtle change had gone through Clayburn's listeners while he was talking. The impending fate of the ranch had rested heavily on every one of these loyal riders. They had made no bones about their intentions of quitting the outfit cold if and when Kruze moved in as their range boss.

97

"For the safety of your own hides," Clayburn wound up, "as well as the future of the ranch, I've got to ride tight herd on you until that beef money is deposited to Broken Key's account at Moon's bank on or before the tenth. Any remarks?"

Spud O'Rourke cleared his throat loudly.

"I reckon," he said gravely, "we all got a stake in this thing. None of us got any whiskey or poker money to fling around even if we went to town."

Charlie Barcus said in a mournful voice, "Sally Nobless is going to be powerful disappointed when I don't show up. Man, she'll skin me alive next time she gets within clawin' range of my hide."

Barcus' words broke the tension. The session broke up on a laughing note, as men started drifting out to their bedrolls. For Clayburn, their reaction to his proposition had not been a surprise. It was significant that he had given no man an opportunity to pull out of the outfit before the trail drive to Highgrade got under way, day after tomorrow. They knew the risks involved and accepted them without question.

At midnight, the incoming nighthawks made the rounds waking up the members of the next shift of circle riders to patrol the sleeping herd. The shift, which would remain on duty until dawn heralded the beginnings of the last day's round-up, included Tuck Clayburn, Spud O'Rourke and young Barcus.

It was a moonless night. The California heavens blazed with myriad stars, and the air over the basin was filled with a mixture of odors—the warm smell of the cattle, the pungency of trampled sage and the scent of night-blooming cactus.

Tuck, saddling a white-stockinged dun from his personal string in the Broken Key remuda, felt his spirits soaring as he contemplated tomorrow's conclusion of the round-up. Every day he could save this side of July tenth made Broken Key's destiny more secure.

He rode out with O'Rourke and the other nighthawks and took up the patrol pattern on the perimeter of the bedded-down herd. On a distant shoulder of the basin a coyote was baying mournfully at the stars; such a sound, magnified by echoes, could easily touch off a stampede.

But the R Bar L herd was bunched close to the lake's edge and up to now, through three nights like this one, had given no trouble. The proximity of water and grass kept bovine tempers honey-sweet. It might be different, crossing Verde Valley and climbing the rocky bottom of the South Fork of the Anviliron toward Wagongap Pass, but they would meet those difficulties as they arose.

Tuck Clayburn soon found himself alone, and had to fight the tendency to doze in saddle. Off in the darkness to his right he could hear Spud O'Rourke crooning an off-key cowboy lament to the sleeping critters. Other riders were patrolling the opposite fringe of the bedground.

An overcast was drifting in off the desert from the Panamints, blotting out the stars one by one. It was not a cloud-cover that promised rain, but more a condensation of the air's moisture when the cold zones of the upper stratosphere mingled with the summer heat rising from the badlands.

Summer Range was at seven thousand feet, and a chill

breeze came down the basin. Tuck pondered whether or not to break out his slicker from the cantle roll.

He reached in his shirt for the makings, then put the hunger for a smoke out of his mind. The change in weather had subtly altered the mood of the herd; the sudden spurt of a lighted match might spook some wakeful herd bull and touch off a——

Suddenly Tuck jerked erect in saddle. The shifting breeze brought to his unbelieving ears the muffled drumming of hoofbeats. Riders, quite a body of them, were hammering down into the basin from the north.

"What darn fools could be——"

Tuck broke off. The riders could not be Broken Key men. They were coming from the direction of Rafter J, but Frank Jessup would have no reason to put night-riders on the trails this high up in the Lavastones, at this time of night.

Whoever they were, Clayburn sensed that they were coming fast and recklessly down the slope toward the lake, straight for his bedded herd.

The Broken Key ramrod reached for the gun at his hip. Every instinct in him was keyed for trouble.

Who those riders out of the night could be, he had no immediate notion. The thought struck him that they might be a platoon of cavalry working down from Fort Mono on cross-country night maneuvers, sweeping into Summer Range basin behind some dog-soldier captain who wanted to make the next bivouac in time for breakfast.

Clayburn put spurs to the dun, intending to beat across the basin and head off the oncoming riders before the herd was turned into a juggernaut of destruction. Broken Key couldn't afford a stampede—it would throw them back two or three days rounding up strays.

Spud O'Rourke was a shadow off to the left as Tuck skirted the muddy flats rimming the receded lake shore. Already the sleeping cattle were stirring and an old herd bull began to bawl nervously.

And then the gunshots came.

Bore-flashes rippled like sparks along a fanned-out arc beyond the dimly-seen white canvas of Farley's chuck-wagon. Clayburn pulled his dun to a bucking halt, hearing the wasp-like whine of rifle bullets crisscrossing the sky overhead.

"Herd raiders!" Clayburn yelled into the night, a blind, unreasoning wrath making his blood run violently. "We're bein' jumped by rustlers!"

That was it. There could be no other explanation for this senseless shooting, this unprovoked night attack. All spring, Fred Locke and Tuck Clayburn had realized that Randie's choice stock might be bait for a long-looper raid before this summer drew to a close.

Tuck hauled his carbine from saddle boot, levered a shell into the breech, and opened fire on the oncoming, unseen riders, aiming at their gun-flashes.

The night was suddenly a howling pandemonium. Gun-fire and shouting voices mingled with the slow-mounting thunder of cloven hoofs and clattering hocks and rattling brush as the bedded-down herd broke into uncontrolled stampede before the onrush of horsemen.

A break in the overcast momentarily flooded the chaotic scene with starlight and Tuck saw the black shapes of

101

anonymous riders pounding in on the flank of the bolting herd, rounding the far end of the lake.

He saw Spud O'Rourke spill from saddle, target of a converging fire. Clayburn emptied his saddle gun in a wild counter fire, knowing the chances of hitting a target were remote in this shifty light.

Swinging his horse around as the immediate surroundings were blotted out by the bolting shapes of R Bar L steers, Tuck spent the next ten minutes out-riding the stampede, knowing if his dun stumbled and threw him he was finished.

Above the cacophony of bawling cattle and rumbling hoofs he heard men, Broken Key men, yelling in anguish. The camp had been over-run. Clayburn flashed by Flapjack Farley's chuck wagon, dismayed to see that it had been overturned by hurtling beasts, and wondered if any of Broken Key's crew had been trampled to death in their bedrolls.

The dun carried him clear of the steers milling around the waterhole and scattering across the basin flats. The raiders had come from the north and, their fiendish chore completed, would probably be quitting the Summer Range over the same ridge.

He gave his horse its head as he found himself lost again in a dusty maelstrom of cattle and saddleless horses which had broken their picket ropes.

There was no more shooting, and the shouts of his men were behind him now. Gradually the fast little dun pulled out of that hazardous ground and the grade tilted up, telling Clayburn that his horse was scaling the north slope of the basin.

He saw riders ahead of him, off to the right and further away to the left, westward. Close to a dozen in all.

They would be members of the stampede crew, instinct told him. Raiders high-tailing out of the basin, melting into the darkness, their damage done.

Clayburn felt sick. Broken Key's carefully gathered herd was scattered to the four winds. Only dawn would reveal how heavy a toll of human and animal life had been taken during these brief minutes of horror in the night.

This could mean Broken Key's ruin. That was Clayburn's uppermost thought as he kept his dun hammering up the north slope, determined now on tailing one or more of the night riders until daylight gave him a view of a target.

In this darkness, he could be mistaken for one of the raiders. Ahead, Broken Key men were rallying on the ridge crest, shouting to each other unintelligibly.

Reloading his Winchester at full gallop, Tuck Clayburn gained the ridge top, gradually losing the sounds of disaster from the basin.

Suddenly a rider loomed up from a shallow barranca paralleling his own route. There was enough light for Clayburn to recognize Charlie Barcus' snow-white pony and his gaudy red-striped shirt.

He risked shouting the kid's name, and saw the rider pull in facing him.

"That you, Chuck?" Clayburn called out, gun palmed as he reined up alongside the cowpuncher.

"Boss? What in hell happened down there?"

Clayburn detected the agony in Barcus' voice. Before he could reach out to grab the kid, the puncher slumped and fell from the stirrups on the opposite side of his *blanco* gelding. The pony reared, trumpeted, and galloped into the darkness, stirrup leathers slapping.

Dropping down beside Barcus, Clayburn touched the kid's white shirt and felt the sticky warmth of blood. He fumbled a match from the snakeskin band of his Stetson and lighted it between cupped fingers, to see the bubbling bullet hole punched through Charlie's breastbone.

Blood was frothing Barcus' lips as the match went out. He was babbling incoherently, but Clayburn caught one intelligible phrase: "It's nice dancin' with you, Sally. You look perty as a new red wagon tonight, for a fact."

By the time Clayburn could light another match he knew Charlie Barcus had crossed the Divide.

Cursing into the night, the Broken Key ramrod climbed back aboard the dun, backed away from Barcus' limp shape on the ground, and headed north, picking up the snare-drum rattle of the raiders' getaway farther along the Lavastone heights.

A fresh thought came into his mind, driving out his rage and sorrow at young Barcus' death: who but Kyle Kruze could have ordered this raid tonight? And if so, how had Kruze learned the purpose of Broken Key's round-up on the remote, lofty floor of Summer Range? Who had spied them out and tipped his hand to the spider who crouched in his web over at Wagonspoke?

Who but Cloyd Weber? They only had the lawyer's word that he had quit Kruze——

chapter 9

DAY'S first ruddy gleam over the Amargosa
Desert flats found Tuck Clayburn sitting on his winded dun
on a high knob of ground that marked the northeast
corner of Broken Key.

He had lost touch with the raiders about two-thirty in
the morning, when a mild sandstorm had whipped up. But
he knew that for ten miles the ambushers had traveled in a
general northerly direction after leaving the high basin.

Since that was all he had to go on until sunrise, Tuck
Clayburn had pushed on in that direction.

Now, picking out landmark by landmark as the day's
light tipped the Panamints and the Furnaces, the Argus and
the Cosos and finally the high Sierras, he watched the
countryside fade from indigo to mauve and finally to a
baked-out, tawny yellow-gray.

A California sunrise, especially in summertime, was something to exalt a man's soul. But this morning, Tuck's eye
was not on the beauty of a new day's birth. He was searching for some track or trace of the riders he had pursued before the short-lived sandstorm had struck. He saw no sign
whatever.

Across Verde's depths, the Furnaces climbed terrace by terrace to meet the skyline, the countless canyons spilling their alluvial fans out into the valley, in places almost touching the eastward-thrusting residue from the Lava-stones.

At this time of day the notch of Wagongap Pass, scene of a reborn gold rush, stood out clearly; Tuck imagined he could see the smoke haze from Highgrade's chimneys. Leading to the pass were the twin canyons of the Anviliron River, the North and South forks, forming an arrowhead pointing toward the site of the gold excitement. On the ridge dividing the two canyons could be seen the dim loops and switchbacks of the old Borax Road to Death Valley, filled with traffic again after years of virtual abandonment.

To the right about five miles away, lay Anvil Mesa, with Broken Key's buildings standing out starkly in the oblique sunlight. Directly ahead, roughly the same distance, Wagonspoke's east-facing windowpanes speared dazzling points of light across the distance.

All this country, a thousand square miles of it, was gashed with dry arroyos and desert sinks, white potash deposits that had once been lakes, timbered slopes and sandy wastes. It was made to order for outlaws to hide in; a regiment of troops could melt from view in any one of a thousand canyons and barrancas.

The only movement to break the painted-picture stillness of this California scene was a feather of dust crawling along the Borax Road beyond Wagonspoke, a jerkline string of mules dragging tandem-hitched freight wagons into the mountains. One of Gabe Garbie's supply trains hauling trading stock to Highgrade, most likely, Tuck thought.

The sharp edge of despair lay on Tuck Clayburn as he put his exhausted horse down the flinty slope of this foothill spur, through a gate in Broken Key's drift fence, and on down the valley's slope toward Wagonspoke.

He was as close to Broken Key as he was to the town, but he dreaded riding over and breaking the news of last night's calamitous events to Randie. There would be dead to bury and maybe a wagonload of injured to haul to Doc Ashton's makeshift hospital in town. Randie's herd—he didn't even want to think about that.

Uppermost in his mind now were the need to get Doc Ashton started out to Summer Range, and the off chance that while in Wagonspoke he might cut the sign of some of the riders who had been responsible for last night's disaster.

Approaching the cowtown, Tuck picked up a pattern of fresh hoofprints quartering the sage flats toward the settlement from the same direction he had left the Lavastone footslopes. He counted a dozen horses, closely bunched, and his range-wise eye sorted out signs in the dust which told him the horses had been hard ridden.

"They laid down this sign since the sandstorm blew itself out," Clayburn muttered through cracked lips. "It could be the bunch who stampeded us. It has to be——"

He followed the hoofprinted lane through the stunted sage and mesquites, knowing he had picked up the trail too late. He saw where the riders entered the wagon road approaching Wagonspoke from the west, but here the tracks became hopelessly confused in the churned volcanic soil.

Riding into Wagonspoke's outskirts, Clayburn sized up the horses rolling in the silver dust of the big corral beside the Lariat Livery, one of Kruze's enterprises. A man could easily tell if a horse had been pushed hard and fast during the night just past, even if a hostler had curried it down.

But this stock lazing in Kruze's corral seemed rested. Passing the black archway of the main barn, Clayburn had a fleeting, end-on view of its double row of inside stalls, and saw that no saddle stock were feeding there. It was extremely unlikely that the raiding party had tarried on its way through town.

As he was passing the adobe jailhouse at the corner of the courthouse plaza a voice hailed him. He turned to see Sheriff Arnie Algar at his office door, unlocking for another day's tour of duty.

Algar was a Verde Valley pioneer of the same generation as Doc Ashton and Fred Locke and Clem Moon. He had packed a star in Indio County for longer than Clayburn's span of life.

Clayburn pulled over in front of the jail building. Algar was well into his seventies but he carried his back ramrod erect and only his tobacco-stained handlebar mustache, snow white now, gave any true indication of his age.

The gravity in Tuck's eyes shut off Algar's customarily jocular bantering. "You look like you been tusslin' with a nightmare, Tuck," he said earnestly. "Not another try at dry-gulchin' you, I hope?"

Clayburn gave Algar a brief summary of last night's depredation at Summer Range, without telling him what the scattering of Randie's herd meant to the future of Broken Key. He wound up by asking Algar if he had heard a body of horsemen ride into town before sunrise.

"I sleep like a saw goin' through a log," the starpacker said. "If anybody rode into Wagonspoke after midnight, I

108

wouldn't know it. The night marshal didn't report anything out of the ordinary when I et breakfast with him just now."

Clayburn said, "No use your riding up to the basin to scout for sign, Arnie. The wind wiped out any tracks. I haven't got much to go on—except I think the raiders came out of Wagonspoke."

Clayburn wheeled his dun and started down the street. Algar called after him, "How'd it happen you boys were gatherin' beef this season o' the year anyhow?" Clayburn made no reply.

Riding on to the bank building, Tuck headed upstairs to Paul Ashton's office. He found the medico at breakfast in the room off his laboratory and recited his story in the expressionless voice of a man near the frayed end of his string. Ashton had his kitbag packed and his hat on before Clayburn was finished.

"Bloodshed and violence," the old doctor commented. "Human nature gets hard to tolerate after fifty years of it, son. I hope I won't find too much work to do out there."

Clayburn watched the doctor depart and then returned to the main street. The town appeared totally deserted; hitchracks were conspicuously empty, except for a half-dozen cow ponies tied in front of the post office, next to Kruze's Montalto Casino. The gold rush at Highgrade had left its mark on the town to an amazing degree.

Clayburn rode across the street to look at the post office rack. He dismissed each horse in turn until he came to a leggy buckskin whose flanks were crusted with dried, dust-browned lather.

Without halting his own mount, Clayburn spotted a detail which started his pulse racing. This particular buckskin's fetlocks were caked with dried mud of a vivid brick-red color. And the pony's exhaustion indicated that it had been ridden hard recently.

The red mud gave Clayburn the proof he had been hunting. Only on the pulverized lava-dust rim of Indian Lake, at Summer Range, was there any red-colored earth moist enough for a horse to sink into fetlock deep.

Leaning from saddle, Clayburn glanced at his own pony's feet. Identical-colored mud crusted the dun's fetlocks. Both horses had slogged through the marshy fringe of Indian Lake last night——

Clayburn pulled into the alley between the post office shanty and Kruze's gambling den and dismounted. After ground-tying his horse, he climbed over the post office porch railing and sat down on one of the benches there.

From here he could spot any rider who might come to claim the buckskin. The color of that horse's coat roused another memory in Clayburn—the tuft of buckskin horsehair Tweedy had found on the day of the attempted ambuscade at the pothole where he had slaughtered the four crippled steers. It was within the range of possibility that the sharpshooter who had attempted to gun him then had ridden the same horse on last night's raid.

I'll dab my twine on at least one of those renegades, Tuck thought wearily, and maybe between me and the sheriff we can find out if Kyle Kruze was behind last night's stampede.

Clayburn was convinced that Kruze had engineered the Summer Range tragedy. No one else would have any motive for bringing disaster on Broken Key. How Kruze had gotten wind of the proposed trail drive to Highgrade,

110

he could not know. And he would probably never know—unless he could force the owner of that buckskin to talk. The pony carried no brand.

He rolled a cigarette and pulled the biting smoke into his lungs with relish. It helped him fight off sleep. His belly throbbed from hunger but he dared not leave his post even for a cup of coffee.

He heard the squeak of hinges on the batwing doors of Kruze's place. The sound brought him instantly alert. A moment later one of Kruze's house men—Trig McCoy, hired to keep the peace inside the Montalto—strolled past the corner of the building. Midway across the alley he paused to yawn and stretch. McCoy showed every evidence of being bone-tired.

The way the saloon bouncer was dressed this morning sent the blood racing through Tuck's veins. He wore apron-style *armita* chaps and high-heeled boots, hardly the costume he would have been wearing if he had spent the past night on police duty in the barroom.

Clayburn flicked away his half-smoked cigarette. He leaned forward as McCoy stepped over the high wooden curb of the plank sidewalk, walked along it past the post office without spotting Clayburn, and headed toward the hitchrack.

Clayburn came to his feet when the saloon bouncer started to loosen the reins of the muddy-footed buckskin.

He had seen enough. Loosening a six-gun in holster, he vaulted the post office rail just as McCoy was hooking an ox-bow stirrup over the saddle horn preparatory to taking up the slack in his cinch.

McCoy heard Clayburn's boots strike the plank walk and

111

he turned full around. Clayburn noticed McCoy's start of recognition, saw his eyes widen with startled wonder for a fraction of a second. Then his features went blank and inscrutable behind the mask he habitually wore.

"Yes, Trig," Clayburn said softly, "I survived your little surprise party up in the Lavastones last night."

McCoy reached up carefully to pick a stub of brown-paper cigarette from his lower lip. His unblinking eyes had not left Clayburn's. His manner betrayed no concern whatever.

"How's that?"

Tuck moved in closer, saw McCoy's facial muscles tense as he moved away from the hitchbar, dropping the bridle reins. His big hands fell loosely at his sides, fingertips brushing thonged-down holsters.

"You've been out riding, Trig," Clayburn went on, deliberately needling Kruze's paid gunhawk. "This is the second try you've made to get me in the past few days. Once at that pothole with your 'scope-sighted rifle. Again last night. I'm getting tired of it, Trig."

McCoy muttered, "I don't know what you're talkin' about, Clayburn. You drunk or somethin'?"

"You're going down to the sheriff's office with me this morning, McCoy, and tell me where you picked up that fresh red mud on your pony's hoofs."

Trig McCoy laughed sourly. "You *are* drunk, ain't you?" he said, turning back to his horse. "You're takin' me no place."

And then, without signalling his next move by a tensing of muscle or movement of his arms, McCoy spun back to face Clayburn, his palms slapping both gun butts simultaneously.

112

Tuck saw the flash of sunlight on lifting gun metal. He knew he could not hope to match or beat that draw, not against a professional gunman of McCoy's speed.

Clayburn's splayed fingers hit the butt of his own gun. His holster was not tied down at the toe, in the manner of paid gunslingers like McCoy.

He swiveled the holster on his belt and tripped the gun-hammer with his thumb in one swift, precisely coordinated motion.

The Colt roared down Wagonspoke's empty street. The bullet made a sharp whacking sound as it caught Trig McCoy's left cheekbone, ripped through brain tissue and out the back of his skull.

Pure reflex caused McCoy to complete his double draw. His twin .45s swept up to a level pointing, but the hands which held them belonged to a dead man.

The ear-slamming echoes of Clayburn's single shot bounced and volleyed off the bank building across the street; the thunder of it must have reached every ear in town.

No eye saw the smoke curling from the open toe of Tuck's holster. No witness saw Trig McCoy standing on wide-braced feet, a gun in either hand, a corpse held up for an instant by the locking action of paralyzed muscles.

Clayburn took a backward step as gravity pulled McCoy's guns down. The man's head slumped forward, and its weight put him off balance. He fell, slowly at first, like a hewn tree; then he was lying on his face at Clayburn's feet, spilling his blood on the baked planks of the walkway.

Tuck Clayburn felt like vomiting. This was the first human life he had ever taken.

A window slammed open across the street and Clayburn

113

saw Clem Moon's figure framed there. Somewhere to his left he heard a shout and the sound of a man's boots slogging up the street.

Clayburn turned and stalked back into the alley where he had left his horse. Regret burned through him, regret that Trig McCoy's guilt had caused him to go for his guns, forcing Clayburn to silence the only witness he had to pin the blame for last night's beef raid on Kyle Kruze. Or Cloyd Weber.

He mounted and rode into the street, ignoring Clem Moon's stunned face in the window over the bank. By the time he reached the courthouse plaza, he hipped around in saddle to see a small crowd gathered in front of the post office.

Sheriff Algar had heard the shot and was just now emerging from his office. Long schooling at his job had given him a sixth sense in differentiating between the sound of a gun fired in anger and that of a drunken cowpoke letting off steam.

His eyes held their question as he came down the jail steps toward Clayburn.

"I just shot and killed Trig McCoy," Clayburn told him heavily. "It was self defense, Arnie."

The sheriff blinked a couple of times. "McCoy? A good riddance to the town. How did it happen?"

Clayburn told the sheriff about the evidence of the red mud on McCoy's buckskin.

"Mud of any color," Arnie Algar drawled, "is as scarce as hen's teeth anywhere in the county, this summer."

Clayburn said, "You'll find him up there with a gun in

114

each fist, sheriff. Neither of them fired. I got my shot off first—without drawing my gun."

Algar thumbed a loose gallus strap over one shoulder.

"Otherwise," he drawled, "Doc Ashton would be writin' yore name instead of McCoy's on his coroner's report this mornin'. Any witnesses?"

"None that I know of."

The sheriff scowled dubiously. "That's bad, in a way. McCoy being one of Kruze's men. Almost druther the shootin' had been seen by somebody."

Clayburn picked up his reins. Hunger and lack of sleep made his head fuzzy, yet he could not tarry here in town when he was needed so urgently at Broken Key.

"Sheriff," he said, "I've got dead and dying men over at Summer Range. I've already sent Doc Ashton out. Is it all right with you if I—run out on this other thing?"

The sheriff waved him to be gone.

"If I need any more details of this shootin' than I'll get by examinin' Trig's remains, I'll know where to look for you, I reckon."

An hour later, reaching the foot of the grade which lifted the road out of Verde Valley to the bench where Broken Key headquarters was located, Tuck Clayburn caught sight of Flapjack Farley's chuckwagon, minus its canvas hood, parked on the skyline of the western ridge.

The glasses showed Clayburn that Doc Ashton was in the wagon box, bending over his work. Whether the wagon was being used as an ambulance or hearse, or both, Clayburn couldn't tell from this distance.

Food and sleep were waiting for him at Broken Key, together with the grim business of telling Randie about what had happened last night—and even worse, McCoy's shooting. But he had to know how severe last night's casualties had been, so he left the road and struck out across the sagebrush toward the skylined wagon.

A rider came away from the wagon and met him halfway down the slope. Clayburn saw, with surprise, that it was Ben Tweedy, whom he had sent back to the ranch with Randie the other day to handle the routine chores there during the roundup.

Tweedy had apparently spotted the chuckwagon heading from Summer Range toward Wagonspoke and had ridden out to intercept it, just as Doc Ashton had done.

Clayburn could tell by the grim set of his roustabout's face that he was bearing disastrous tidings.

The two reined up stirrup by stirrup without speaking. Then Tweedy said, "Four dead. Irv Weingross and Ferd Adams got theirs out on the bedground. Charlie Barcus and Spud O'Rourke gunshot."

"Their bodies in the wagons?"

"No room for dead meat. Chip Wayne drove the wagon over. He's got Jim and Fat in the box. Doc is lookin' 'em over. Internal injuries, he reckons. They got trampled in their bedrolls."

Clayburn's stomach churned. These were the men with whom he had eaten and slept and played and worked over a long period of years, all except young Barcus. Trig McCoy had paid the price for last night's bloodshed, but the score was not yet settled in full. It probably never would be.

chapter 10

"How about Flapjack Farley?" Clayburn asked.

A grin broke the solemn mask of the roustabout's face.

"That old mossyhorn claims he slept through the whole shebang. And I wouldn't doubt but what he did. Anyhow, he's makin' up for it this mornin', Chip says."

"How?"

"He's takin' over as your straw boss out at the basin, Chip says. He's diggin' graves for the boys there by the lake where the live oaks grow, while the rest of the crew are out roundin' up the herd again."

Clayburn let his glance slide off Tweedy and up the ridge, knowing he should be riding up there to give Doc a hand and a word of cheer to the injured men. But there was still more news to be learned from Tweedy, and he wanted it all in a bunch.

"How bad did Chip say the herd was scattered?"

Tweedy made an all-inclusive gesture with a bony hand.

"To hell and gone and back again. Into the barrancas you boys been flushin' 'em out of all week. Boys'll be mighty relieved to see you ridin' back with a whole hide, son. Chip said when he pulled out with the wagon, Flappie

117

was half a mind to drag the lake huntin' for your carcass. You bein' missin' was almost as bad as findin' you tromped into the dirt."

Up on the ridge, the wagon was moving again, Chip Wayne in the driver's seat. The team, Clayburn saw, consisted of saddle horses rather than Farley's harness mules. The latter animals had either stampeded or been killed or maimed last night, he decided.

Doc Ashton was removing the two injured punchers to his little hospital in town. There was nothing Clayburn could do for Jim and Fat, not right now.

Tweedy had not asked him one word about what had happened. Apparently Wayne had described the night's horrors. Tweedy said now, "Kyle Kruze was back of it, the boys all know that. Farley had to haul a gun on the crew to keep 'em from sashayin' into town to polish Kruze's plow for him."

Clayburn said heavily, a mental picture of Trig McCoy's collapsing body returning to torment him, "Kruze was back of it, all right, but we'll never be able to prove it. Ben, I want you to ride out to Summer Range this morning. I've got to head home and hit the blankets before I fall out of this saddle."

Tweedy nodded sympathetically.

"What's the score on this trail drive to Highgrade now, Tuck? Another round-up, or have we missed out?"

Clayburn dragged a shaking hand across his eyes.

"That's what I want you to tell the boys. Tell Flappie you're giving the orders out there till I show up this evening. Tell the crew we can still make it, by the skin of our teeth. We had a week's leeway before this stampede came

118

up. Next time we'll be forewarned and there will be no raiders breaking into the basin past our guard."

He picked up his reins and turned back toward the Broken Key road. Ben Tweedy called after him, "Randie already knows the worst, kid. Her and me rode out to meet that wagon. Knew when we saw it headin' for Wagonspoke instead of the ranch that somethin' bad was afoot."

Clayburn felt a sense of relief realizing that Randie would not have to hear the bad news from his lips first.

"Doc Ashton sent her back to the ranch," Tweedy went on. "You'll probably find her fixin' to leave for the basin to help bury Spud and Chuck and the others. She's bad broken up about it, but mostly she's worried about where you disappeared to."

Tuck put his horse into a jog-trot; the animal was too spent for a faster gait.

He was passing the graves of Fred and Molly Locke, where the road cut over the Anvil's rim, when he saw Randie on her palomino, heading for the upper Lavastones.

She was too far away to notice him, so he hauled his Winchester from its boot and fired a single shot at the sky. When the sound of the report reached the girl she swung her palomino around, recognized him, and came spurring back.

They met under the locusts in front of the ranch house. Relief at seeing Tuck alive was too much for Randie and she burst into tears, going at once to his arms.

"Randie, I'm sorry," Tuck breathed in her ear. "But the boys are out there rounding up the herd again. This just slowed us down a few days. We'll make it to Highgrade yet."

119

Randie said in a broken voice, "Poor Spud. And Charlie —with that girl in town he was planning to marry this fall. And Ferd Adams and poor old Irv——They gave their lives for Broken Key, Tuck——"

She pulled herself from his embrace and brushed tears out of her eyes.

"But you're safe," she said. "And very tired and hungry. I'll have breakfast whipped up for you by the time you've turned your horse into the corral, Tuck."

During the course of his meal, Clayburn could not bring himself to tell her of Trig McCoy's death. He remembered how Fred's gunfight with Kruze had upset the girl. She would hear about McCoy soon enough. Nor did he mention Weber's name.

He headed out to the bunkhouse and, too tired to shuck off his cowboots, fell on his blankets and was instantly asleep.

Sundown light was staining the bunkshack windows when Tuck Clayburn was roused by a heavy hand shaking his shoulder. He sat up groggily, to see Sheriff Arnie Algar beside his bunk, with Randie behind him.

One glance at the expression on the girl's face and he was wholly awake, struck by a grim foreboding of what had brought the sheriff out to Broken Key.

"Tuck, I don't like doing this," the lawman said uneasily, "but I'll have to take you back to town. You're under arrest. Kyle Kruze has sworn out a first-degree murder warrant ag'in you. There was nothing I could do but serve it."

Tuck stared at the paper Algar was fishing from his jumper pocket.

120

"You mean—Kruze called my shooting of Trig McCoy a murder?"

The sheriff nodded, misery in his eyes.

"When I got to McCoy, he didn't have guns in his hands like you told me. He wasn't even wearing guns."

Clayburn came to his feet, anger discoloring his face.

"Damn it, sheriff, you know I wouldn't cut down an un-heeled man. Kruze got to the body before you did and dis-posed of McCoy's irons, that's plain enough to see."

Algar scrubbed his boot toe on the worn linoleum of the bunkhouse floor.

"I know. But Kruze has come up with witnesses to that shootin', son."

"Witnesses? The street was empty."

The sheriff waggled his head sorrowfully. "There was quite a crowd around McCoy's body when I got to it. At least two of 'em—Tussie Keller and Red Venable—swore on oath they saw you cut McCoy down in cold blood."

Randie came past the sheriff to take Clayburn's arm.

"You'll have to go down to jail, Tuck, but you won't be locked up for long. I'll get Cloyd to have you released to my custody. He can do it."

Arnie Algar shook his head. "First degree murder ain't a bailable offense in this state, Randie. I'm afraid Tuck will have to roost in my hoosegow until his trial comes up."

Randie said in a hollow voice, "But Judge Heckendorf is out on circuit, up in Bishop or someplace. He won't be back to this end of the county for weeks——"

"Court convenes in Wagonspoke on the fifteenth of July," Algar said.

Clayburn set his jaw.

121

"That's the whole idea back of this trumped-up charge, Randie. Kruze thinks by keeping me behind bars until the middle of July, he can prevent our saving Broken Key. Well, it's up to Flapjack and Tweedy and the boys to call Kruze's bluff."

They left the bunkhouse together, and Clayburn noticed that while he slept, Randie had saddled a pair of horses for their trip to town.

"I'm going with you, Tuck," the girl explained. "I'll talk to Cloyd. He's a good lawyer. He'll help us."

Algar and Clayburn exchanged pessimistic glances. The sheriff noted that his prisoner was still wearing his .45s, and made an embarrassed gesture which caused Clayburn to unbuckle his shell belts and pass over his guns. Algar stowed them in a saddlebag. He had a pair of handcuffs there, but made no move to use them.

Darkness overtook the three of them as they were turning in at the courthouse plaza. For Randie, it was the bleakest moment of her life, even taking into account her father's funeral, when she saw the sheriff usher Clayburn inside the cellblock and heard the clang of an iron door closing.

When Algar came back outside, Randie said frantically, "This is a serious thing, isn't it, Arnie?"

The sheriff looked away. "Clayburn could hang. That's how serious it is, Randie."

In the thick twilight Algar saw the girl staring at him intently, and he guessed at the run of her thoughts when he saw her hand fall to her side, to the .32 pistol at her hip.

"You could put a gun on me and spring yore brother out of my hoosegow," Algar said, "but you'd have to kill me to do it, honey, and even then Clayburn would be on the dodge."

Randie made a choking sound and turned away. She started to run and did not stop until she was hammering on Cloyd Weber's room in the rear of the Wagonspoke Hotel.

Weber had just returned from eating supper in the hotel dining room. Before Randie had finished pouring out her story, she guessed from his expression that the lawyer had known of the forthcoming arrest. His first words, spoken tenderly as he held her hard against him, confirmed her worst dreads of the seriousness of Clayburn's position.

"I'll handle Tuck's defense in court, of course, darling. But I've talked to Kruze this afternoon about the matter. He's got a pretty solid case on Tuck. Witnesses——"

"Witnesses!" panted the girl, pulling free of Weber's arms. "Tussie Keller, Kruze's bartender, and Red Venable, his roulette croupier. Paid perjurers, you mean!"

Weber shrugged. "Their word against Tuck's—the jury will have to decide, Randie."

The girl came to him again. "Cloyd, you have influence on Kruze. If you love me, get Kruze to drop those charges. You could do it. You could tell him you've found witnesses who can swear that McCoy drew first—that it was self defense."

"But Kruze swears McCoy was unarmed——"

"You know he wasn't, Cloyd, and so does Kruze. You've got to bluff that evil man, Cloyd."

A calculating look came into the lawyer's eyes. By nature he had always been a coward, but his love for Randie was real, as vital to his happiness as the fulfillment of his professional ambitions.

He knew he would never find Randie in a weaker moment than now, her defenses down.

Facing her, Weber quickly formulated his campaign. His opening gambit was a defense of his honor.

"Randie, are you asking me to falsify the facts—in order to bluff Kyle Kruze into withdrawing his charges on Tuck?"

Randie averted her eyes. "The means—justify the ends, Cloyd. I would tell a thousand lies to save my brother."

Weber's eyes narrowed. "Tuck Clayburn," he reminded her, "is not your brother, Randie. Sometimes, when I see him looking at you, I think he is a rival for your heart, a man who loves you—and I don't mean in the fraternal sense."

Randie looked startled.

"Then you know how much Tuck means to me, Cloyd. You'll talk to Kruze? You'll trick him, if need be, to call off those perjured witnesses of his? Tuck's life is at stake, Cloyd."

Weber moved closer to the girl, sure of himself now, sure of his own bargaining position.

"If I discard my code of honor—if I succeed in getting Tuck out of that jail tonight—will it make you love me enough to consent to our marriage, Randie?"

It was blackmail disguised as devotion, but Randie was too desperate to analyze the situation. He lowered his mouth to meet hers and kissed her demandingly, his blood fired by her nearness, her surrender.

"I am yours, Cloyd," she whispered when they broke apart.

Five minutes later, Cloyd Weber faced Kyle Kruze in the gambler's private office.

"Kyle, you made a mistake pushing murder charges against Tuck," the lawyer said quietly. "I know why you did it, of course—to keep him from making his cattle drive, in the event he recovers after that raid of yours last night. But complications have developed."

Kyle Kruze rubbed his crippled fist, his eyes warily alert. In times of stress, he invariably turned to Weber, knowing from past experience that his confederate's knowledge of law and its loopholes formed an indispensable part of his operations in Verde Valley. He felt that sensation of comfort now, that sense of having a crutch to lean on, a steadier brain to turn to in emergencies.

"Complications? What do you mean?"

Weber's face was grave. "Algar and Tuck have witnesses to that shooting, Kyle. Witnesses who were afraid to come forward with their version until they heard that Tuck was jailed tonight."

Kruze grinned without conviction.

"To hell with Tuck's witnesses. We can———"

"Those witnesses will shoot your story full of holes when it hits a courtroom, Kyle."

Kruze sagged back in his chair. "What witnesses are they?" he asked finally.

Weber shook his head. "Tuck and Randie and the sheriff swore me to secrecy on that score, Kyle. But they're bona fide."

Anger darkened the gambler's face.. "Whose lawyer are you—mine or Randie's?"

Weber said patiently, "That isn't the point, Kyle. Take

125

my professional counsel at face value—you can't make that murder charge hold up in court. You're trying to railroad Clayburn to the gallows. The town knows it."

Kruze said defiantly, "And I'll see him hang, too."

"No. If you do, Wagonspoke will rebel, Kyle. You are a big splash in this town. But Clayburn has friends, powerful friends. As your lawyer, I have my duty to do here—to keep you from getting too big for your britches."

Kruze pulled in a heavy breath.

"You've already told Randie you aren't my lawyer. How do I know you aren't double-crossing me now?"

Weber made a gesture of impatience. "We've threshed all that out. I've got to make sure of Randie becoming my wife, at all costs. I've got my political future to think about. Don't forget, Kruze, when I go to Sacramento I will be able to help you in big ways. Here in Verde Valley we're playing for penny-ante stakes. If we are to get into the big-money game—we've got to cooperate."

Kyle said thoughtfully, "You think your political future depends on marrying Randie—you think that's so important?"

Weber said earnestly, "It's all important, Kyle. Can't you understand that? Look at me—a cowtown lawyer, a nobody. But as Randie's husband—as the nominal controlling agent of a ranch as important as Broken Key—I'll be an important citizen, Kyle. The world at large need not know Broken Key is actually your plaything."

Kyle's expression changed. He had come to a decision in Weber's favor; the lawyer knew that, the instant the thought entered Kyle's brain. His schooling in psychology had developed a natural talent for swaying jurymen and more than once, in a difficult case, he had seen the tide swing in his favor long before the evidence was in or the opposition's arguments concluded.

"O.K., Weber," Kruze said, reaching for his black Stetson. "I'll take your word for it that you know the best course to take. Much as it galls me—I'll go over to the jail and have Clayburn released from custody. I'll tell Algar my witnesses were intoxicated—that they've retracted their testimony since I swore out that warrant. Is that satisfactory?"

Relief flowed through Weber. He had argued his toughest case and he had won. No judicial decision he would ever gain for a client would equal this moment's triumph in personal importance.

He was thinking, This should put me ace-high with Randie again. It's got to. It was a risky thing, bluffing Kyle——

He was not sure whether he had done the wise thing, lying about friendly witnesses who did not exist. If Kruze ever discovered the truth, Weber knew he was done for.

Heading toward the jail with Kyle Kruze at his side, Cloyd Weber felt a wave of fear—the fear of a man who realized, too late, he was enmeshed in a dangerous alliance.

Neither of them spoke until Weber halted at the hotel. Then Kruze said, "I might as well keep you up to date on developments, Weber. I had a talk with Frank Jessup today —about his beef herd. Let Clayburn go ahead with his trail drive. He's going to have competition, Weber. I'll be entering a herd of my own in that race."

Kruze was gone then, heading toward the courthouse. His words made no immediate impression on Weber. What occupied his mind was that tonight he had cleared his biggest hurdle and that his reward was waiting to be claimed.

He found Randie waiting in his room, her cheeks glistening wet, suspense written in every line of her face.

"It's done, Randie!" the lawyer said exultantly. "Kruze is on his way to Algar's office now. It seems his witnesses were—intoxicated. They swore to a garbled story concerning McCoy's death."

He expected the girl to rush to his arms, to feast him with kisses. Instead, she said wearily, "I promised to be your wife, Cloyd, and I will keep that promise. But you will understand—why I want to get over to the jail to be there when Tuck comes out?"

Weber fought to control the harsh disappointment her words brought him. "Of course."

As Randie started for the door, Weber reached out suddenly to detain her, his other hand reaching into a pocket of his vest.

"Wait just one tiny moment, darling. I want to show you something———"

Randie stared down at the ring in Weber's hand. Even in the dull light of the hotel's ceiling lamp, the magnificent diamond, nested between seed pearls, glittered like liquid fire. Cloyd Weber took her left hand and slipped the betrothal ring on her finger.

"I would have preferred a more romantic setting," he laughed. "Moonlight, and the scent of roses, and all. But———"

Randie Locke's senses reeled. Her rough ranch life had

had no room for feminine fripperies, jewels, perfumes. This diamond had cost Weber a fabulous price, she knew.

"It—it's the loveliest thing I ever owned," she whispered.

After the girl had left, Weber sat down and lighted a cigar, found it distasteful, discarded it and poured himself a heavy bracer of whiskey from the decanter at his bedside. He felt cheated by the realization of the tawdry means he had used in forcing what amounted to a bargain upon Randie Locke.

"As soon as Randie will marry me," Weber promised himself, "we're getting out of this damned country forever."

chapter 11

On the night of July second, aided by an early half-moon, the Broken Key trail herd moved off its home range and began its passage across Verde Valley. This leg of the drive was without grass or water and would have been untenable to drovers and cattle alike in the day's heat.

The round-up in Summer Range, following the stampede, had taken eight full days before Tuck Clayburn's tally book showed the necessary five hundred head. This left a scant eight days for the Highgrade drive, and while no man hinted it openly, none of Clayburn's crew believed there was an outside chance of meeting Kruze's deadline at the Wagonspoke bank.

The night raid at Summer Range had dissipated Clayburn's precious cushion of reserve time. From here on to trail's end, they had no margin for rest layovers or unforeseen delays.

Randie rode in Flapjack Farley's chuckwagon a mile ahead of the herd, with Ben Tweedy driving the hoodlum wagon behind. Their first camp would be inside the South Canyon of the Anviliron, where grass and water could be found in fair supply.

130

Clayburn was riding point. His punchers along the flanks and bringing up the drag were armed to the teeth and had been warned to open fire on any unidentified body of horsemen who might approach the herd's line of travel in the moonlight.

During the past week, Clayburn and Randie had pored over the map of Indio County, double-checking the available routes to Wagongap Pass. They had three choices. One was the Borax Road, which dated back to the pioneer '60s; it followed the backbone of the rugged spur separating the twin forks of Anviliron River, designated on the Army maps as Alkali Ridge.

But in all probability the road would be clogged with gold-hunters bound for the new bonanza. Even Randie's small herd could jam such a road for a mile at a stretch, therefore it was out of the question.

The two branches of the Anviliron converged at the mile-high level to form the narrow corridor of Wagongap Pass. The river was a mere trickle at this season, its flow vanishing entirely when it reached Verde Valley's thirsty wastes.

"Last time I scouted this slope of the Furnaces," Tuck had informed the girl, "was when Fred and I went deer hunting up there the first winter of the drought. I know the North fork has the easiest grade, but very little graze until you hit the springs at Emigrants' Meadows, halfway to the Pass. The South fork will take a day's drive longer, but is our best bet for water and graze. Either way has its disadvantages."

Randie Locke had said quietly, "Crowding the herd, as we will have to do to make our deadline, we've got to consider the condition of the cattle, Tuck. We can't deliver gaunted-out specimens to Mose Kaploon. Not when Garbie is promising us ten times the market price for each steer."

Had it not been for the heartbreaking delay caused by the second round-up, Clayburn would have scouted the two routes flanking Alkali Ridge in advance, and chosen the better one. But there was no time for that now. The decision, the win-or-lose gamble, rested squarely on the judgment of these two.

Ultimately, Randie left the decision to Tuck.

"The South Fork it is, then. And heaven help us if winter landslides have blocked off any part of that gorge. We've got to have every break in our favor——"

Midnight found the herd passing the outskirts of Wagonspoke. Tuck and Chip Wayne were riding point; yipping Broken Key hands were popping the knotted ends of ropes to keep strays from bolting the flanks.

They left the town behind them, a town fully aware, by now, of the drama underlying this unprecedented mid-summer trail drive.

When daylight broke over the parched land, the herd had reached the foot of South Canyon and had moved inside the gorge mouth, out of view of Verde Valley.

Randie and Flapjack had breakfast awaiting the crew. When he had finished bolting his food, Tuck Clayburn selected a fresh horse from the cavvy and saddled up.

Randie came over from the chuckwagon to inquire what he was up to, knowing Tuck had not averaged four hours' sleep a night since Sheriff Algar had released him from the Wagonspoke jail. His need for rest was written in the harsh furrows seaming his cheeks, in the blue pockets under his

132

eyes. He had not shaved in a week or had the shirt off his back.

"I'm going to scout up-canyon," Clayburn answered the girl's question. He noticed that she kept her left hand behind her, and he sensed the reason. He had first glimpsed Cloyd Weber's engagement ring on the moment of his emerging from the Wagonspoke jail, and Randie's intuition told her what a shock that diamond had given Clayburn.

"You've got to rest," the girl protested. "You're not resuming the drive until the middle of the afternoon."

He shook his head. "If I find the canyon blocked up ahead, by a rockslide or quicksand or something, I'll have to locate a side draw over the ridge to the North Canyon."

There was nothing Randie could say to that. The chore was necessary. All the hands were as gaunted-out as Clayburn. As herd boss, scouting each day's drive in advance was his unshakable responsibility.

Climbing into saddle, Clayburn said gravely, "I want you to go back to the ranch now, Randie. Or stay in town with Mrs. Algar or somebody. I can't have a girl on this drive."

She knew he was anticipating a Kruze ambush, but she answered, "You need every hand you can get. I will relieve Flappy of his cooking chores. With Broken Key at stake, you couldn't keep me from this drive. Besides, these cattle belong to me, remember."

Clayburn picked up his reins. "Assume we save the ranch—as we will. You'll be marrying Cloyd Weber before the month is out——"

"No, Tuck. I promised Dad I'd wait till my next birthday and I am going to wait. Cloyd—is resigned to that."

133

"All right," Clayburn said. "What becomes of Broken Key? You'll be moving to Sacramento next spring. Maybe clear out of California eventually, if Cloyd's political luck holds out. You——"

"Broken Key," she reminded him, "is your ranch, not mine."

"I'm deeding it back to you. It's your money that will be redeeming Fred's debts."

"I won't accept the deed," she retorted. "You're forgetting something, Tuck. You belong on Broken Key. Dad knew what he was doing, willing it to you. You are as much Fred's son as I am his daughter, and always have been."

That eternal sister-brother angle, he thought morosely. Aloud, he said, "You belong on Broken Key too, Randie," and, without giving her a chance to answer, spurred away from the camp.

Long after she had retired to her blankets in the box of Tweedy's hoodlum wagon, snatching what sleep she could before the herd got under way again that afternoon, Randie pondered that abrupt departure of Tuck's, smacking as it did of jealousy.

She sensed an undercurrent of unrest in him. She felt, somehow, that her impending marriage to Cloyd Weber was coming between them, destroying the warm rapport and boisterous camaraderie they had known through their growing-up years together.

The herd covered a scant six miles of canyon bottom between noon and sundown of July the third. Tuck Clayburn had been spared further scouting trips up the gorge when he encountered old Sam Scalee coming back from Highgrade with another pair of pokes filled with gold dust and nuggets from his claim.

The South Canyon fork of the Anviliron was unobstructed, Scalee reported, to its junction with the North Fork at the west end of Wagongap Pass. Scalee knew this terrain like a book.

By noon of the Fourth of July, Tuck figured the trail drive was a good ten miles ahead of schedule. At this rate, they would reach Garbie's holding ground on the mountain meadow outside of Highgrade by the morning of the eighth.

The return to Wagonspoke, down-grade all the way, and following the old Borax Road down Alkali Ridge, could be negotiated by a rider easily by late afternoon of July ninth.

Broken Key's debts became due at noon on the tenth. That gave him all the leeway he needed to settle Fred Locke's accounts at Moon's bank. For the first time in six years, the ranch would be free of indebtedness. Its future greatness would depend solely upon the amount of winter rainfall and the snowpack in the high Lavastones.

Eating his noon meal in the saddle, a mile in advance of the plodding herd, Tuck was joined by Randie, who had persuaded old Flapjack to let her take over his cooking duties, freeing Flapjack for drover's work.

They were short-handed on this drive, due to the loss of men during the raid on Summer Range and the necessity for leaving a skeleton crew at Broken Key during their absence.

"Happy Fourth of July, Tuck!" the girl sang out, rounding a bend of the canyon and spurring up alongside Clayburn. "Our own Independence Day is less than a week off. Everything's going grand. We're going to make it."

Tuck took a swig from his canvas waterbag. He scanned the cliffs of the canyon moodily.

"Things are going too good," he said with a pessimism which was alien to his nature. "I don't like it. I'm going to double our guard at night. We're overdue for another attack from Kruze."

Randie's face sobered. Always in the back of her mind was the knowledge that any turn of the canyon might bring the smash of drygulch guns. In this restricted passage, a stampede could wipe out the crew, trapped between the creek and the cliffs. It was a risk she shared with the men.

But in spite of their apprehension, the day was uneventful. The following morning, Randie again joined Tuck as he scouted the trail.

"We're doing fine," he said, "but I can't help wondering what Kruze is up to."

"It isn't like him to take this lying down." She admitted her own secret fears. "He's undoubtedly planning something."

Tuck gestured toward the north rimrock. The white-hot California sky was vaguely obscured with thin brown clouds up there.

"That dust up yonder," Tuck said. "It's been bothering me all day. Too heavy to be coming from wagon traffic on the Borax Road. First arroyo we come to, I'm crossing the ridge to find out what's causing it."

Two hours and one mile farther up the canyon, Clayburn spotted a break in the north wall and, threading his way through the bawling herd which was strung out along the

136

narrow south bank of the river, he forded the shallow Anviliron and headed toward the crest of Alkali Ridge.

Leaving the arroyo, he found himself on the heavily-traveled Borax Road which was now the main artery of supply for Highgrade. As far as he could see, up or down the grade, eager gold hunters were moving toward the new diggings.

Some were afoot, carrying picks and pans; others were on muleback, or in creaking two-wheel carts. There were buggies and buckboard wagons, an ancient Studebaker prairie schooner with a man's family under its patched hood.

By now the news of Highgrade's rebirth as a gold camp had had time to spread from the Pecos to the Pacific and from Canada to Mexico. It was drawing a growing tide of treasure-hungry humanity into the Furnace uplands.

Most of these bonzana hunters would find only disillusionment and poverty, or death, at the foot of the rainbow that beckoned them from halfway across a continent. But each one of them was a prospective customer for Gabe Garbie's butchershop at the boom camp.

On the crest of Alkali Ridge between the two canyons, the mysterious dust cloud which had turned the westering sun into a dull copper disk was more pronounced than it had been from the trail drive.

Its source seemed to be somewhere in the pit of the North Canyon. When he had made sure of that, Tuck Clayburn was struck with a numbing prescience of disaster.

He spurred off the wagon road and followed a cactus-spined hogback to its sheer jump-off into the Anviliron's north fork.

Five hundred feet below and a mile down-canyon, he made out the russet sprawl of a thin line of cattle advancing in his direction. From this distance, Clayburn could see the moving specks that were cowpunchers on the flanks and riding point.

That strung-out column of beef cattle was plodding up the almost-dry bed of the north fork of the river, lifting a dust pillar which flattened out thousands of feet overhead.

Clayburn was swept by a giddy sensation. Someone else was pushing a herd toward Highgrade to cash in on that fabulous beef market!

For Broken Key, this meant a trail race. Tuck knew that despite the inferior grass conditions in the bottom of the North Canyon whoever was there had a twenty-mile advantage over Broken Key. Twenty miles meant two days of driving time.

Unbuckling a saddlebag, Clayburn took out his cavalry binoculars and focused on the oncoming herd, searching for brands which might identify the source of that rival beef.

"*Rafter J——*"

That oncoming herd, which stood better than a fifty-fifty chance of beating Broken Key to Garbie's market, belonged to Fred Locke's long-time neighbor, Frank Jessup.

Jessup must have gotten wind of the potential riches to be gleaned by supplying the booming gold camp with fresh meat, and had put his own Escondido Valley cattle on the trail.

Studying what riders he could see through the heavy dust, Clayburn convinced himself that the drovers were members of Jessup's crew. Jessup himself was riding point.

Anger lifted in him, anger and bewilderment and a

138

crushing sense of being burdened with another load when he was already carrying more than any man could bear.

Yet he knew such an attitude was unjustified. Frank Jessup was having a hard time making ends meet, the same as Broken Key. If he could tap the rich market of the gold camp ahead of Randie's herd, he had every moral and legal right to do so. He had his own spread to save from Kyle Kruze's bank.

The Rafter J cattle, Tuck could see, were hungry and thirsty, shedding tallow every mile they traveled. Tuck had chosen wisely and well in gambling that forage conditions would be more favorable on the south side of Alkali Ridge, thanks to a heavier run-off of water from the Anviliron.

But even if Jessup's herd reached Highgrade reduced to bone and hide and gristle, their presence would cause a collapse in the beef market. Their arrival would handicap Garbie in making good on his deal with Broken Key; as a matter of fact, according to the verbal terms of the deal, Garbie would cancel negotiations with Broken Key altogether. Jessup was as much Garbie's friend as Fred Locke had been.

The fundamental law of supply and demand would force Garbie to lower his bid to equal whatever Rafter J established in Highgrade. The net sum would undoubtedly fall far below the minimum of eighty-seven thousand dollars which the bank required of Broken Key.

Tuck cased his glasses, a bitter frustration replacing his first feeling of resentment and anger toward Jessup's competition.

By sundown, Jessup's herd would pull abreast of Broken Key. The race would be won or lost by the herd which first reached the bottleneck of Wagongap Pass, where the river canyons met. From there on across the summit of the Furnace Range to the site of Highgrade camp, there was only room for one trail herd between the funneling granite walls of the narrow Pass.

It boiled down to a case of winner take all.

There is only one thing to do, Clayburn told himself, wheeling his pony around and heading back toward the Borax Road. I've got to keep my cattle moving all night tonight and tomorrow and tomorrow night, even if we have to drop the stragglers behind. If Rafter J hits the Pass five minutes ahead of us, Kyle Kruze has won the Broken Key.

When Tuck rejoined his herd two hours later, he found that the news of Rafter J's making a race of this drive had already reached Randie and the cook. The messenger was Cloyd Weber, who had ridden from Wagonspoke to break the news.

Farley's chuckwagon had withdrawn into a side pocket of the canyon to repair a loose hub and Weber was there with Farley and Randie. Tuck's first glimpse of the bitter despair in the girl's eyes told him that she had written this drive off as a lost cause.

Her words were a hammer blow for Clayburn.

"Kyle Kruze is challenging us with a Rafter J herd, Tuck. You've seen the herd? It isn't Jessup's. Not any more. Kruze foreclosed on Rafter J a week ago. Cloyd just told me."

Clayburn slumped in saddle, staring down at the two.

"Kruze has seven hundred animals in his herd," Weber said. "As soon as I got wind of his drive, I thought I ought

140

to ride up here and let you know what you're up against."

Tuck stared at Cloyd for a long moment. Then he said harshly, "Is Kruze with the herd?"

The lawyer shrugged. "I couldn't say. He's nowhere around town. Perhaps he has gone on ahead to Highgrade to arrange for a buyer. At any rate, Tuck, you might as well abandon this drive of yours. There's no use in further punishing your men or your cattle. Kruze will beat you to the Pass by a full day at the least."

Clayburn's eyes narrowed, raw suspicion filling them. He could not get out of his mind the possibility that Randie's fiancé might have been the cause of the Summer Range stampede, despite Weber's insistence that he was no longer Kruze's attorney. Was this what the lawyer had ridden up from town to do—influence Randie to call it quits?

Clayburn edged his horse off the trail to make way for a random jag of cattle. The canyon was a pandemonium of bawling steers and clattering hoofs on gravel and the shrill yip-yip-yipee of cowpunchers, none of them yet aware of the competition overtaking them a few miles to the north.

"We are not calling this race off," Tuck snapped angrily. "I'm driving by night, no matter how many strays we lose."

Weber blinked. "Since the cattle are Randie's, perhaps that is for her to say."

Randie shook her head despairingly. "Tuck is in charge. If he thinks we stand a chance to beat Kruze's outfit to the Pass, we drive by night."

Clayburn's glance shifted to Cloyd Weber, then back to Randie.

"I'm riding on ahead to Highgrade," Tuck said suddenly. "I want to find out first-hand if Kruze is there trying to sew

141

up the beef market. I want you to ride up to the point and give Tweedy orders to keep this herd moving all night, understand? I'll be going by way of the Borax Road."

Before the girl could answer him, Clayburn had wheeled his horse and was lost in the dust.

A moment later Randie Locke felt herself being swept into Cloyd Weber's arms, his mouth pressing hungrily on hers.

The untimeliness of his overture, at a moment when her personal world was on the brink of ruin, outraged the girl and she broke free, slapping her left hand impetuously across his cheek. A sharp point of the diamond in her engagement ring left a red track across his flesh. Over by the wagon, old Farley gave an approving snort.

"Randie!" Cloyd choked out. "What——"

A deep revulsion took hold of the girl then. Hardly with conscious volition, she felt herself ripping the diamond off her hand and flinging it at the man before her.

"It's no use—it's no use, Cloyd," she husked out, choking back her tears. "I can't marry you. We—we aren't suited for each other."

Weber turned ash-white. He stooped to pick up the costly ring from the dirt and stood turning it over and over in his hands.

"You're tired and angry," he said finally. "You can't mean this. You gave me your promise——"

"But under what circumstances, Cloyd? Can't you see— how empty things are between us? I—I agreed to marry you in good faith, I know that. But think of the pressure I was under—Tuck in the shadow of a hangrope—I—I guess

142

I was snatching at straws. Offering myself to you in return —for what you could do with Kruze———"

A hot flush suffused Weber's cheeks. He screwed the square-cut diamond onto the little finger of his left hand with savage jerking movements, not knowing what he was doing, his whole nature surfacing in his crazed eyes.

"It's Tuck," Weber bit out. "It's been Tuck all along———"

Randie Locke turned away, burying her face in her hands, her slim shoulders shaking.

"I love him—I guess I've always loved him," she admitted, more to herself than him. "I've been blind, looking on him as a brother. Oh, forgive me, Cloyd, please forgive me———"

When she got herself under control and turned around, it was to see Flapjack Farley regarding her sympathetically from his perch on the chuckwagon. There was no sign of Cloyd Weber or his livery-stable horse.

"He's lit out, honey child," old Farley said paternally, his eyes shining with a deeper inner joy. "You won't ever regret it, Randie. Not ever. Take an old man's word for it."

chapter 12

KEEPING to the old Borax Road, Tuck Clay-
burn reached the site of the old Wells Fargo relay station
midway down the length of Wagongap Pass. After water-
ing his horse there, he withdrew to a timbered spot away
from the road to make his night camp.

Throughout the night, his rest was disturbed by the constant rumble of wheeled traffic moving toward the gold
fields. At dawn, after breakfasting from the dried corn and
jerky and canned peaches in his saddlebags, the Broken Key
ramrod pushed on to the summit. By seven o'clock he was in
sight of the old ghost town of Highgrade.

Several years back, on his last deer hunt in this country
seven thousand feet above sea level, Highgrade had been a
sprawling collection of abandoned and rotting buildings.
Only about twenty-odd recluses had lived there, including
old Mose Kaploon, who had kept Garbie's branch store
operating for the benefit of the sheepherders and prospectors who peopled these mountains.

Seeing it now, Clayburn was hardly prepared for the
change the gold strike had wrought in Highgrade. The
mouldering board-and-bat buildings, dating back to the

original strike of '66, were still here; but for a mile along the mountain divide a city of tents and dugouts, covered wagons and packing-box huts had sprung up as profuse as wildflowers after a wet winter.

Highgrade had leaped from a town of twenty to nearly three thousand souls in less than a fortnight; its peak was yet to come.

Scalee's new strike—actually made by an anonymous Panamint Indian buck whose identity was already lost to history—had been made in Shirttail Canyon, five miles southwest of the original Highgrade mine. Clayburn already knew that every inch of its meandering twenty-mile length had been staked out in mining claims. The same was true of the other canyons which corrugated this roof-tree of the Furnace mountain system.

The confusion of the scene baffled Clayburn. Chinamen were working the vast tailing dumps of the old '66 diggings. Carpenters were busy throwing up saloons and store buildings.

Claim jumpers and pickpockets, professional cardsharps and fancy women from Tonopah and Goldfield and Las Vegas were here in force, adding color to the swarming street which followed the uncertain line of the divide.

Smoke was spewing from the lofty brick stack of the old thirty-stamp reduction mill on a slope overlooking the town; it would shortly be in operation, as wagons began hauling in ore.

Gamblers and saloonmen, pimps and their courtesans, run-of-the-mill desperadoes were swarming on Highgrade and vicinity like a host of vultures, gathering to prey on the hard-working muckers.

It was an old story, common to Alder Gulch and Cripple Creek, Oro Fino and the Mother Lode, Tonopah and Bullfrog and Panamint City and Skidoo and all the other mining camps the West had known. But seeing it with his own eyes, range-bred Tuck Clayburn could not comprehend it.

Five minutes after entering the camp, Clayburn learned that a Vigilante Committee had already been formed. The corpses of no less than four claim-jumpers swung from the historic old hangtree in the center of the camp, a grisly warning that Highgrade had its own rough law to cope with violence and outlawry.

Clayburn passed canvas-roofed gambling halls, earthen-floored, where games were going at full blast, even at this early hour. Watered whiskey was being dispensed at a dollar a shot. Assayers were doing a land-office business with their hastily imported cupels and crucibles, balances and acid bottles. A sod-and-adobe bunkhouse was advertising bed space at ten dollars a night—"No Vermin at this Altitude."

When Clayburn finally reached the weatherbeaten, false-fronted shack housing Garbie's branch store, across the street from the Overland Telegraph building, he was confronted by a padlocked door and a crudely lettered sign reading CLOSED TEMPORARILY FOR RESTOCKING. BUTCHERSHOP OPENS JULY 11.

At the back of the building he found old Mose Kaploon, Garbie's storekeeper, feverishly unloading supplies which had just arrived in a Conestoga wagon. Kaploon was a man in his seventies, possessed of a monstrous belly and a face

146

that bore the scars of forgotten fistfights dating back to the original boom of the sixties.

He barely had time for a handshake with Clayburn.

"Can't hire help for love ner money, Tuck. The town's gone hawg-wild. Gold-crazy, like before. I offered a Panamint buck twenty dollars just to unload them kegs of nails Garbie sent up from Wagonspoke. He spit in my face. Thinks he can scratch a nugget out of the grassroots anytime he wants to. I tell you, it's hell."

Then the old man realized he had overlooked the significance of the Broken Key cowpuncher at his back door.

"By grab, Gabe telegrapht me you were bringin' up a jag of beef on the hoof. I can convert 'em into hard money as fast as I can carve off the steaks. Yore herd here already?"

Clayburn said, "Another three-four days. Where do you want 'em bedded down?"

Kaploon mopped his bald skull with a bandanna.

"Best grass is in Wildrose Flats just this side o' the Pass. Them steers will hardly have time to build a cud before I'm out there butcherin' 'em, though—steaks ain't to be had fer love ner money in this camp."

Tuck nodded, fixing the location of Wildrose Flats in his head. He said, "Seen anything of Kyle Kruze in town?"

Kaploon shook his head. "No, but that don't mean a thing, my nose bein' to the grindstone day and night. Highgrade's worse'n a tromped-on anthill. Son, I bet I gross a thousand bucks a head the first day after I get one of yore Broken Key steers on my choppin' block. A slab o' bacon, last I had, went for its weight in gold dust yesterday. I tell you, the town is stark ravin' loco. And where one man rakes in five hundred for an afternoon's gravel scratchin', fifty won't make enough to resole their boots."

Tuck decided the time had come to broach a touchy subject. He explained as succinctly as possible Kruze's bid to out-race Broken Key's herd to the camp.

"If those scrawny Rafter J critters hit town first—what then, Mose?"

The old storekeeper waggled his head sorrowfully. "We cain't let that happen, is all. There's a dozen stores sprung up in town, mostly Nevada people, gettin' their supplies from as far off as Reno an' Salt Lake City. They'll jump at the chance to bid on Kruze's beef. I doubt if I could compete with 'em, either, onct the market is flooded with meat. These miners are crazy, but they'll only put away so many steaks."

Kaploon had no more time to devote to small talk. After diplomatically parrying the old man's hints that he help unload the Conestoga's freight, Clayburn made his way back to the main street, keeping a sharp eye out for sight of Kyle Kruze.

He crossed to the Overland Telegraph office and found it to be the only place in town that was not jammed with gold-hunters. The dyspeptic old operator on duty there, one of Highgrade's permanent citizens since the '66 boom, told Clayburn that his wires were kept busy with New York and San Francisco brokerage houses wanting to keep posted on the status of the new Highgrade boom, but otherwise he was not being overworked.

"Only thing worries me," the key pounder acknowledged, "is that some jackleg muckers may take a notion to chop down a few telegraph poles to shore up their prospect holes.

Good timber is hard to come by in the Furnaces, and lumber that's bein' shipped in costs more'n a sane man would pay."

Tuck dispatched a short message to Gabe Garbie in Wagonspoke, acquainting the trader with the status quo, and then made a brief sortie in hopes of buying a sack of oats for his pony. Feed for livestock, however, was unobtainable at any price in the camp, and at one o'clock that afternoon, the Broken Key foreman left Highgrade for the Pass.

So far as he knew, Kyle Kruze was nowhere in the camp; but locating him in all this frenzied congestion would be like hunting for a marked fish in the ocean.

The issues were clear enough. Kaploon would buy Rafter J meat from Kruze if Jessup's herd won the trail race; Garbie's deal was not binding in that event. Kaploon was a natural-born trader and would drive a hard-hearted bargain if he could.

Darkness overtook Clayburn on the Borax Road outside the cliff-walled slot of the Pass. The air was so full of dust that it was impossible for him to determine the relative positions of the two herds in their opposite canyons.

Opposite Emigrants' Meadows, Jessup's first real water hole on the way up, Clayburn turned south into Gunsight Wash, the largest side-draw entering his own canyon. He had not covered five miles below Gunsight when a Broken Key nighthawk, Chip Wayne, challenged him from the darkness.

After identifying himself, Clayburn demanded worriedly, "I don't hear the herd coming?"

"It's bedded down for the night, boss."

149

Clayburn reeled in the saddle. "Bedded down? I left orders for Tweedy to keep pushin'——"

Wayne said despondently, "You can only push a critter so far on a steep climb like this, Tuck. We couldn't of kept 'em movin' if we'd called down thunder and lightenin' to prod 'em."

Sick with disappointment, Clayburn headed down-canyon until he saw Flapjack Farley's cookfire burning its orange hole in the darkness, laying a shimmering track across the shallow river. The Broken Key herd was bedded down somewhere farther below.

All of the crew not on herd duty were asleep in their bed-rolls at the base of the cliffs. Randie Locke was nowhere around, which meant she had probably retired for the night in the hoodlum wagon.

Clayburn off-saddled and picketed his horse out to graze. He had not eaten since morning and he was poking around the campfire's cooling kettles when Flapjack Farley crawled from his blankets under the chuckwagon.

"I didn't locate Kruze up in camp," Clayburn gave his report. "What's the situation with the Rafter J herd? Any-body cross the ridge to check on 'em today?"

Farley said glumly, "Randie did, just at dark. Kruze's beef passed us this mornin' and bedded down a good five mile closer to the Pass than we are, Tuck. At Emigrants' Meadows spring."

Clayburn devoured his food in glum silence. Finally Farley spoke from his bedroll again, "They overtook an' passed us without havin' to drive all last night like we done, either."

The ramrod's shoulders lifted and fell.

"We stand to lose the race to the Pass, at this rate," he acknowledged heavily. "Kaploon wouldn't commit himself to holdin' up for us."

He tossed his dishes in the wreck pan, went to the hoodlum wagon and got his own bedroll. Then he carried his bedding to the edge of the talus and sat down to shuck off his boots. Weariness was in him, to an extent that he could not feel despair at the turn this trail race had taken during his absence.

Ben Tweedy, sleeping nearby, roused when Clayburn touched a match to a cigarette and, recognizing the ramrod, said apologetically, "I called a halt to this night-drivin' when Randie told me where Rafter J got durin' a day's easy travelin' up that other canyon, Tuck. I figger they'll hit the fork of the Pass by late tomorrow. It was no use killin' our stock. It would take a miracle to beat Jessup now."

Tuck Clayburn nodded, a vast soul sickness keeping him mute.

After an interval, Tweedy spoke again from the shadows.

"You talk to Flappie?"

"Yeah."

"He tell you about Randie an' that fancy-pants dude?"

Clayburn pinched out his smoke, instantly alert.

"What about 'em?" The panicky thought struck him that he had not heard the girl breathing in the hoodlum wagon, that probably she had gone back to Wagonspoke to get married.

"You better ask Flappie," Tweedy said, turning over in his blankets and beginning to snore.

Clayburn scrambled out of his blankets and made his

151

way over to the chuckwagon, shaking the bony old cook awake.

"Tweedy says you know something about Randie and Weber——"

Farley coughed, propping himself up on one elbow.

"By rights, you ought to hear about it from Randie, not me."

"Hear *what?* Give out, you pestiferous old fool!"

Farley sighed deeply. "Well, she give Weber back his diamond ring. Right after you pulled out for Highgrade. Said marryin' him was out o' the question, them bein' too misfitted for each other. I could of told her that, three year ago."

Tuck Clayburn felt a heady exhilaration as if he had just swallowed a pint of raw whiskey.

"And that wasn't all I heard Randie say," Farley went on slyly. "What it was, you'll have to git from Randie, though. Warn't right for an old gaffer like me to eavesdrop on her bustin' her engagement, but I got ears like a elephant."

Clayburn pawed around in the darkness, found Flapjack's bald head, lowered his hand and got a firm grip on the cook's stringy beard.

"Don't clam up on me," he warned, "or I'll rip your whiskers out by the roots, Flappie. I'm all ears myself."

Farley slapped indignantly at the ramrod's hand.

"Well, she said something to the genril effect that she was in love with you, Tuck, an' not from a sisterly p'int of view, neither."

"You aren't hoorawin' me, Flapjack?"

"I've spoke my piece, damn you. Now leggo my chin

fodder afore I whup you to a frazzle with a wagon tongue. Can't a workin' man git his night's rest without bein' pestered by a lovesick young buck?"

Tuck Clayburn let go of the cook's whiskers and got to his feet, feeling like a kid again.

"Flappie, if it wasn't so dark, I'd give you a big kiss right on that bottle nose of yours."

"You just dast to try it," snorted Farley virtuously, "and I'll slap yore sassy face!"

chapter 13

Exhaustion and mental strain had caught up with Tuck Clayburn at last, for he slept without stirring while the crew breakfasted only a short distance away.

"We'll ketch blue blazes for lettin' him sleep in," Ben Tweedy commented at sunrise, "but the kid's string is frayed out. Question is, Randie, what's the program for the day? Keep these mossyhorns shovin' along toward Highgrade? Or head 'em home?"

Randie, who had prepared most of the breakfast by lantern light in spite of Flapjack Farley's protests, realized that the crew believed the race was lost but were waiting for quitting orders to come from her.

It was a difficult decision to make. Randie knew they were two days short of this canyon's junction with the mouth of Wagongap Pass, where the river forked. She knew Kruze's Rafter J herd had bedded down last night on Emigrants' Meadows grass and that it could reach the river's fork by tomorrow noon at the latest, possibly by tonight if Jessup crowded the pace.

The Pass, rather than Highgrade itself, was the actual finishing line of this trail race, owing to the peculiar geographical and geological formation of Wagongap. It was a slot, not a valley.

Despite the fact that the Anviliron River used the Pass as its waterway, erosion had not carved that channel. Wagongap was actually a prehistoric earthquake fault, a fissure in the Furnace Range, the pit of which had been filled in over thousands of years by alluvial silt deposited by the river.

This fill-in left room for the Anviliron, except for the flash floods or freshets caused by spring thaws, and a ledge wide enough to accommodate a single wagon track, with occasional wide spots where traffic could pass.

Where a trail drive of cattle was concerned, however, the situation was analogous to a single-track railway with side tracks on either side converging on the main line. The North and South Canyons were the side tracks on which the rival cattle herds were advancing toward the one-way track of the Pass. Whichever herd made it to that main line first, automatically had clearance to the gold fields at Highgrade.

"I wasn't awake when Tuck got in last night," Randie said. "Did he tell you anything about today's drive, Flappie?"

Old Farley, for some reason the girl could not divine, was blushing furiously.

"We talked some when Tuck got in, yes," Flapjack said. "He was sore as hell about Tweedy holdin' up the night drive, o' course, but he didn't arger too much about it. I reckon he wants us to hit the trail ag'in, though. Tuck ain't the stripe to give up until the last slim chance is behind him."

Randie joined the feverish activity at the remuda, saddling her favorite mount, the palomino which her father had brought from a breeding farm at San Gabriel for her eighteenth birthday.

She was riding up-canyon, noting that Tuck Clayburn was still asleep as she passed the campsite, when Ben Tweedy overtook her. As acting trail boss in Clayburn's absence, Tweedy should have been superintending the resumption of the drive. Instead, he had delegated that job to someone else in order to act as Randie's bodyguard.

"Where you goin', headin' up-canyon?" the roustabout demanded. "You think bein' a woman makes you bushwhack-proof?"

The girl, knowing Tweedy too well to take offense at his possessive tone, gestured toward the north.

"Up to the Borax Road for a look at the situation at Emigrants' Meadows. I've got Dad's telescope with me this time. I'm curious to know if Kruze is with his drive."

Tweedy spurred his hammerhead roan to a canter to keep pace with Randie's palomino. It was the first hint that the roustabout intended to come with her, and his presumptuousness annoyed her.

Her real motive in getting away was for self-communion. The dissolution of her betrothal to Cloyd Weber day before yesterday had not been the result of a fit of temper; her decision had been months in the making.

Originally, as a girl of seventeen, she had been attracted to Cloyd by his handsomeness, by his impeccable manners and his gallantry toward women. After living among rough men—diamonds in the rough, she knew them to be—for her entire life, Cloyd Weber's polish, his charm and his ambitious plans for the future had had a strong appeal.

But this morning, she found herself in the role of a

156

woman who had jilted a man. She had gone back on the promise she had made him the night Weber had been instrumental in getting Tuck Clayburn out of jail.

She knew that Cloyd Weber would come back from Wagonspoke, probably today, entreating her to take back the diamond she had thrown in the dust at his feet. That outburst, especially since it had been witnessed by old Flapjack, brought her an acute sense of shame and self-condemnation in the broad light of a new day. She had behaved childishly, in a fit of anger because Weber had been impulsive enough to kiss her in Farley's presence. She had even lost her control so far as to have slapped him. Such cheap theatrics were beneath her.

She knew she would apologize to Cloyd Weber when she saw him next. But she was equally sure that she would not be persuaded to become his fiancée again. Her world and his were poles apart, a thing she could realize if Weber couldn't.

There was the matter of her affection for Tuck Clayburn, an affection which she had taken for granted during her adolescent years, but which she now, for the first time, recognized for what it was—the ripening love of a mature woman for a man who suddenly loomed as her heart's choice for a husband.

"Ben," Randie Locke said with a touch of her annoyance showing in her voice, "you're needed back at the herd. I wish you wouldn't tag me around like I was a little pigtailed brat."

Tweedy's gnome-like face turned mahogany color under his gray brush of whiskers.

"Many's the time I've daddled you on my knee, Randie.

I ain't tryin' to stick my horns into your affairs, but you ain't ridin' up this canyon alone, nosir."

They halted their horses to square off for argument. Randie gestured to the pearl-handled .32 Smith & Wesson revolver she wore at her belt. She had worn it, at her father's insistence, ever since she was old enough to ride out on the range alone, as a protection against rattlesnakes or other common emergencies.

"Ben, you taught me how to use this gun, so you know I can take care of myself. Now please go back. I—I sort of want to be alone this morning."

Tweedy continued to shake his head.

"Clayburn wouldn't want you traipsin' off alone, not this mornin' 'specially, reckon," the oldster insisted. "Too much chance o' Kruze havin' drygulchers planted up in that belt o' jack pine timber we're comin' to."

Randie opened her mouth to give Tweedy a final, irrevocable order to leave her, but before she could bring herself to tongue-lash the old man, Tweedy spurred on ahead of her.

"I'm honin' to take a look at Kruze's beef myself," he said. "Come on. You couldn't shake me off any quicker than ifn I was a cocklebur, reckon."

Randie surrendered to the lovable old coot and spurred the palomino along after him.

A mile farther up the canyon they came to the Gunsight Wash turn-off and headed up its brush-bordered path, noting the in-bound tracks Clayburn's pony had made last night on his return from Highgrade.

That single trail seemed to relieve old Tweedy; it was

proof that no Kruze riders had taken this side draw over the ridge during the night.

They gained the ridge when the sun was an hour high and crossed the Borax Road, heading for the high point of land overlooking the North Canyon and the green oasis of Emigrants' Meadows.

Reaching it, both Tweedy and Randie were momentarily shocked speechless by what they saw on the Meadows bench below.

The grass-covered bench, fed by artesian springs half a mile away from North Canyon, was piebald with the bright patches of Rafter J cattle, peacefully grazing.

Smoke curled from a cookfire, out of sight under the crest of a rocky ridge, marking the rival camp.

Three or four cowpunchers ranged the outer limits of the meadows, which had been a favorite camping ground of overland emigrant trains during the 'forties and 'fifties.

"Why—Kruze isn't putting his herd on the trail today, it would seem," Randie Locke broke the silence between them. "I'd expected him to be well up the canyon by this time of day."

Ben Tweedy cranked a scrawny, shotgun-chapped leg over his saddle pommel and began shaping a smoke, his eyes studying the grazing herd down there.

"This don't make sense, Randie," the old man muttered finally. "Why should Kruze stop a day's drive short of the Pass, knowin' what it means to beat Broken Key?"

Randie, busy studying the Meadows through old Fred's brass telescope, made no answer. She recognized one of the herd guards as white-haired old Frank Jessup himself.

"On the other hand," Tweedy drawled, swiping his

159

tongue along his brown-paper cigarette, "the grass at the Meadows is the first chance them Rafter J critters have had to work up a cud since Jessup put 'em on the trail. Could be Kruze was forced to hold over a day. Knowin' he's got better'n a fifteen-mile jump on our herd anyhow, restin' 'em up is good strategy."

Randie passed the telescope to her roustabout, a frown of concern creasing her forehead.

"Ben, I don't like this," the girl said anxiously. "Kruze knows he can't let us block off the Pass ahead of him. He's up to something."

Tweedy's raw, bloodshot eyes looked grave. He passed the spyglass back to Randie and wheeled his horse toward the Borax Road.

"I'm gittin' back for a pow-wow with Tuck," he said. "I got a hunch Kruze will have his gun-toters up from Wagonspoke today, all primed to wipe us out from ambush somewhere in that timber between us and the river fork. Them jack pines are thick as the hair on a brush. Made to order for bushwhack. Kruze could pick us off like settin' quail."

When they got back to the Borax Road crossing and were heading for the upper end of Gunsight Wash, Tweedy suddenly raised an arm and pulled in his horse. Randie halted the palomino obediently, wondering what the roustabout was up to.

"I want you to stay right here until I get back, Randie," Tweedy said, avoiding her eyes. "You got a clean sweep of the wagon road here, where you could see any riders Kruze might send acrost Alkali Ridge into our South Canyon."

Randie nodded, pretending not to see through Tweedy's motives for keeping her from accompanying him to the

160

Broken Key herd. Tweedy expected trouble when the cattle worked their way into the heavy timber ahead, and he wanted her well out of it.

"All right, Ben," she acquiesced. "I'll keep a stirrup eye peeled for you."

Tweedy vanished into the brushy depths of Gunsight Wash, quirting his horse recklessly in his haste to make a report to Tuck Clayburn.

Although it was not yet eight o'clock in the morning, the heat and dust were becoming unbearable here in the open. Randie dismounted and led her palomino to the nearest shade, a wind-slanted bosque of junipers overlooking Gunsight Wash's entrance.

She off-saddled and was watching the slow approach of a Concord stage toiling up the grade from the direction of Wagonspoke when a sudden clatter of hoofbeats directed her attention back to the road.

Two riders were emerging from the North Canyon side of Alkali Ridge and were heading into the Gunsight Wash trail.

They were Kyle Kruze and Cloyd Weber.

As the brush closed over them again when they entered the Wash, shock brought cold moisture to Randie Locke's cheeks. What was Weber doing in Kruze's company, this far from town? Why were they headed in Broken Key's direction?

Day before yesterday, when she had broken off their engagement, she had assumed that Weber would go back to Wagonspoke to sulk and lick the wounds to his pride for a day or two, and then be back to offer her his love again.

Now it would seem that he had merely joined forces

161

with Kruze, in which case he would take out his hurt and jealousy on Broken Key. Randie was positive that the two were riding into South Canyon to reconnoiter Clayburn's trail drive.

Not quite sure what she should do in this situation, Randie saddled hastily and led the palomino back to the road. The fact that Kruze was with Weber—and that they had no doubt just come from the rival bedground in Emigrant's Meadows—had sinister implications.

Randie put her palomino down the Gunsight trail, fighting the thick brush and the dust left by the two riders' passage ahead of her.

Twenty minutes later, emerging into the cliff-hemmed corridor of South Canyon, she saw where Kruze and Weber had turned left, up-canyon toward the east, away from the advancing Broken Key cattle drive. Their tracks were plain in the riverbank's mud.

Oblivious to possible danger involved in overtaking the pair, Randie headed her palomino up the canyon. Two hundred yards from the exit of the Wash, she rounded a sharp-angled bend of the canyon to find herself facing a five-acre clearing surrounded by heavy jack pines. The timber crowded in close on the Anviliron's bed ahead, closing off her view of the canyon.

Then she caught sight of Cloyd Weber, alone in the center of the heavily-grassed canyon park. He had dismounted alongside the bank of the river. She saw no sign of Kyle Kruze.

The grass was belly-deep to a cow, burned dry as tinder by the hot weather that had prevailed here since April.

Spurring into the clearing, Randie headed toward the

162

lawyer. He was engrossed in something, unaware of her approach. As Randie rode in, she saw that he had a lariat tied to his saddle horn. To the hondo end of the rope he was tying what appeared to be a gunny sack.

Touching spurs to the palomino's flanks, Randie pushed her mount through the heavy grass toward the river. Morning sunlight shafting through the crown growth of the jack pines flashed like quicksilver off a stream of liquid which Weber was spilling from a bottle onto the gunny sack.

Weber could not hear the approach of Randie's horse through the dry grass because of the subdued roar of the Anviliron plunging over the nearby rapids. It was the jingle of a bit ring which caused him to spin around and face her.

Weber's face instantly screwed into a contorted mask of guilt and shame and fear. The raw odor of kerosene reached Randie's nostrils as the bottle dropped out of his hand. What Weber was doing was all too plain. The oil-soaked burlap told its own story.

"*Cloyd!*" the girl cried out aghast. "You were soaking that gunny sack with coal oil—aiming to drag it through this dry grass and set it afire—so the wind would carry it into that timber! You were going to start a forest fire ahead of our cattle drive!"

Weber broke the shackles of paralysis which had frozen him in this moment of discovery. His eyes held the wild look of a trapped animal, at once depraved and defiant.

"Randie," he choked out, "I'm in this too deep to back out now. I want you to listen to me. Kruze's beef herd had to hold over a day—they needed rest, feed. Kruze has a dozen gunmen here besides Jessup's crew. Kruze would

163

have laid an ambush for Broken Key today if I hadn't talked him out of it—for your sake."

The disillusionment in Randie's eyes sickened the man. He went on numbly, "Fire could gut this canyon—stop your herd without endangering any human life. I—I had to promise to touch this fire off—in order to hold back Kruze's dry gulchers, Randie. Can't you believe that?"

Randie Locke was staring at him with the same revulsion she would have given a diamondback rattler. She saw anger replace the humility in the lawyer's eyes as he started searching his pockets for matches.

"Damn you, woman, you drove me to this—you've outlawed me———"

Randie heard Weber's voice taunting her as if from a remote distance. Her brain reeled as she saw him clawing matches from the box. One flaming sliver dropped in this dry park would be prelude to conflagration.

"I won't let you do it," she cried frantically. "I'll kill you first!"

As she spoke, Randie pulled the .32 revolver from holster, thumbing the knurled hammer to full cock.

She saw Cloyd Weber shrink back before the menace of her gun. And then, from the black timber across the grassland, a Winchester cracked above the whisper of the river rapids and Randie felt her palomino stagger from the impact of a steel-jacketed .30-30 slug drilling its skull. Kyle Kruze was in those pines.

The horse fell sidewise into the grass as if its legs had been cut out from under it by a scythe. The nickel-plated .32 flew from Randie's hand as her body struck the turf.

She did not have time to jerk her boots clear of stirrups.

164

A stab of pain went through her left leg, piphoned under the palomino's thousand pounds of dead weight. She felt the death-throes run through the magnificent horse in jerking, diminishing spasms, its lifeblood staining the grass like red paint.

"Cloyd—Cloyd, I'm pinned down——"

Weber did not appear to hear her cry. Through a haze of agony she saw him fire the oil-soaked gunny sack with a match, saw him leap into saddle without turning in her direction and spur off toward the rimming timber, the torch dragging through the dead grass behind him.

A billowing coil of smoke and dust followed Weber. Randie heard the ominous crackle of flames springing up along Weber's trail. She wrenched desperately at her vise-gripped leg, and then her senses skidded over the rim of a spinning black funnel and she was lost in its vortex, plunging into a void where pain and death and treachery had no meaning.

Kyle Kruze, sitting his big bay saddler, was booting his carbine as Cloyd Weber plunged his horse into the pines, the timber growth crowding him down to the ledge overlooking the river's foaming rapids.

The lawyer's eyes held a frenzied look as he loosened the dallies of his trailing lass'-rope and hurled it into the river. The horror of what he had done was eclipsed by the realization that he had deserted Randie Locke, possibly to be cremated by the flames he had started.

"Kyle—I've got to go back there—your shot dropped the horse on her leg."

Kruze's gold-tipped teeth flashed in the forest's twilight.

"My shot saved your miserable life, you mean. She was all set to cut down on you."

"But I—I still love that girl. I'm going back, Kyle———"

Weber swung his horse around, putting his back to the big gambler. Before he could spur his mount forward, Kruze lifted Colt from holster and its heavy discharge filled the canyon with clashing echoes.

The impact of the point-blank bullet striking him between the shoulder blades lifted the lawyer out of the stirrups. He struck the rim of the ledge and plummeted to the white water below, the river snatching its victim and carrying Weber's body along its bottom, lost to Kruze's view.

For a long moment, Kruze sat his saddle, staring at the river, half regretting his impulsive shot. But Weber had outlived his usefulness to Kruze, and it would have been dangerous to have allowed him to ride to the girl's rescue. As it was, Randie Locke would die and Kruze's part in this tragedy would never be known.

The advancing flames forced Kruze to swing his horse around and head up-canyon toward the Pass. He spurred the bay into a run as wind-borne sparks peppered the conifers ahead of him and threatened to turn this timber into a raging inferno.

chapter 14

Tuck Clayburn plunged his horse up-canyon, threading through masses of plodding R Bar L steers, taking to the river shallows when the trail was blocked off ahead of him.

Punchers jeered him good-naturedly as he fought to reach the point of the herd, adding to the ramrod's embarrassment at having overslept for the first time he could remember. The drag-end of the herd had been passing the camp by the time he had bolted the breakfast left warming on the cookfire coals when Flapjack Farley pulled out with the chuckwagon.

He felt disgraced. But it was Flappie's fault for giving him the news about Randie's break-up with Cloyd Weber and thereby making it impossible for him to get to sleep last night.

Nearing the front end of the herd, Clayburn caught sight of Ben Tweedy riding in the opposite direction on the deer trail on the other bank of the river. He shouted at the roustabout, intending to tell off the codger for not waking him, but the rumble of hoofs and the heavy drift of dust kept Tweedy from spotting him.

Finally Clayburn located Farley driving the chuckwagon up ahead. That reminded him that Randie should have been driving the wagon, freeing Flapjack for drover's duty.

He overtook the wagon and shouted to the old gaffer above the jangle of pots and pans, "Where's Randie this morning?"

Farley yelled back, "Her and Tweedy went over the hump for a look at how Kruze's herd drive is goin', boss."

Clayburn started to turn back, then thought of something.

"I just saw Tweedy high-tailing back down the canyon. Randie wasn't with him!"

Farley bobbed his head. "I know. Somethin's rowelin' Ben. Rode past me like the devil was after him. Yelled somethin' about Kruze holdin' his herd on the Meadows this mornin' instead of hittin' the trail. He was on his way to tell you."

The significance of that astonishing news was lost on Clayburn. Obviously Ben Tweedy, whom he had given explicit orders to keep an eye on Randie for the duration of this drive up the canyon, had left the girl somewhere ahead.

Passing the chuckwagon team, Clayburn headed up the river-bank as fast as the horse could manage the constant upward grade. He was out of sight of the chuckwagon and following herd when his nostrils picked up the odor of wood smoke.

Alarm stabbed the Broken Key trail boss. Fire could be terrifying in a dry season like this. Parched conifers could go up like gunpowder, out-running the fastest horse. The scourge of forest fires, set by lightning or neglected campfires, had already denuded most of the Furnace slopes of timber.

Wild unreasoning terror gripped Clayburn as, rounding the canyon where Gunsight Wash opened from the north, he saw the pink flicker of fire on the rolling underbelly of thick smoke clouds rising above the canyon rims dead ahead.

Had Randie ridden on up the canyon after Tweedy left her? If she was beyond that fire, she could be asphyxiated even if the flames failed to overtake her.

He tried to assure himself that Randie must still be up on the ridge, where she had gone with Tweedy to scout the rival herd this morning. Then he saw the fresh pony tracks leading out of Gunsight Wash and recognized the unusually small hoofprints of her palomino. No other horse he knew of would leave a trail like that. She had gone up-canyon.

His cowman's instinct told him to dash back to warn his point riders to halt the oncoming herd. If the lead bull scented this forest fire ahead, he could put the entire herd into a stampede. If the wind shifted and funneled the conflagration down-canyon, the crew would have its hands full saving their own lives in the cliff-hemmed trap, disregarding the herd.

But concern over Randie blocked out all else in Clayburn's mind now. He put his horse past Gunsight Wash, having to fight the animal as they came closer to the pall of ugly ochre-colored smoke beginning to fill the canyon from rim to rim.

Following a game trail around a canyon bend, Tuck reined up, sick despair running through him.

Facing him was a five-acre expanse of what had been

169

grassland an hour ago. Beating him in the face now was a wall of superheated air. Directly ahead, in plain view across the clearing, was the flank of the fire itself.

Piñons and jack pines had already been stripped of their resinous needles and were being reduced to charred snags, burning from roots to crowns like giant torches. The wind was pushing the fire up-canyon, the high cliffs confining it to this belt of timber.

There was no time to think about how the blaze had started, or what it meant to the trail race which his men had already written off as lost to Rafter J's rival herd across the ridge.

Under other circumstances, Clayburn would have been concerned only about these calamities. The fire was gutting the canyon all the way to the mouth of Wagongap Pass. It would be an impossibility to get the Broken Key cattle through that inferno of smouldering stumps and snags; it would take weeks for the deadfalls to burn themselves out.

But Broken Key's crowning stroke of misfortune did not matter now. Clayburn's sole concern was for Randie's safety. Was it possible that she had been ahead of this fire when it broke out, and so had a chance to out-run it to the river fork above timber line? Or had she turned back to warn her drovers?

Tuck's saddler was bucking violently, panicked by the roar of the flames beating up the canyon ahead, spooked by the hot pressure of the air. Tuck knew he had reached dead end in his search for Randie. No living thing could enter that blast furnace of burning conifers ahead. The heat in the air was lifting steam off the Anviliron's rapids to his left.

170

He started to rein his horse around, knowing his own life was in peril if the wind shifted. The horse reared, and as Tuck grabbed leather to keep from being thrown from saddle, he caught sight of something in the middle of the grassy clearing that demanded investigation.

At first glimpse it appeared to be a big boulder lying at the blackened edge of the fire. Then he saw a flash of bright metal that could be the silverwork on the pommel of the saddle he had given Randie for Christmas last year.

Tuck pulled his horse around in a tight circle now, whip-sawing the reins brutally, raking his mount's flanks with the gut hooks. He forced the crazed horse into the clearing, sunfishing every foot of the way.

Then a billowing eddy of hot air swirled over the clearing, flattening the sun-cured grass like a bed of kelp under an ocean wave, and he saw that the rocklike object was a golden-maned palomino lying on its side—its rider pinned under its barrel.

"Randie!"

As Tuck shouted the girl's name his horse jerked the reins from his hands, swallowed his head like a rodeo bucker, and as Tuck rocked violently in saddle, swapped ends and arched his back like a bursting spring.

Clayburn kicked his boots free of stirrups. He felt himself cartwheeling through space. Then the cushioning buffalo grass loomed up to engulf him as he landed on all fours.

Dazed, Clayburn pulled himself to his feet. His horse had already vanished through the smoke, heading away from the fire.

He was afoot. If the wind changed he knew he would be

surrounded by an impenetrable barrier of flaming forest in a matter of moments. The nearby river was his only escape.

Clayburn jerked his bandanna neckpiece over his face and slogged through the belt-high grass toward the fallen palomino, heat burning his exposed flesh, every breath sheer torture.

Then he caught sight of Randie, lying inert, one leg pinned under the weight of the dead palomino.

Sobbing her name through the folds of the bandanna, Tuck fell on his knees beside the girl. At first glance he thought she was dead; her face was chalky and her body moved slackly as he got an arm under her.

Then he saw the strong beat of a pulse on her throat and knew she must have fainted from lack of oxygen.

He saw the blood-spattered grass, the bullet hole bored neatly through the white patch on the palomino's head, and knew why she had been trapped when her horse fell. Whoever had gunned the palomino must have been the cause of this fire.

Clayburn's head was splitting. The danger from proximity to a major fire, he realized numbly, was from smothering rather than the actual flames.

Straddling Randie's unconscious form, Tuck seized her saddle by horn and cantle and, the desperation of the moment lending him strength, pulled upward on the dead weight of the horse's carcass.

Cords swelled on his neck. He felt the strain of overtaxed muscles and tendons as he struggled to free Randie's leg of its anchoring weight. His senses were swimming when he finally got the girl's knee and ankle out from under the palomino.

He had no recollection, later, of lifting the girl and stumbling through the dense grass toward the river; the next he knew he was skidding and sprawling down the steep bank of the Anviliron.

Whirling gusts of wind peppered the river's ripples with burning débris, bringing up little splashes and hissing spurts of steam.

Then he was stumbling across the steaming strip of mud and into the river, sprawling headlong to immerse himself and the girl completely in the cool flow of the Anviliron.

The shock of it revived his senses and he braced the spike heels of his Justins into the gravel bottom, lifting Randie's head out of the sluggish current.

Randie's body jerked convulsively, slipping from Tuck's grip, and in the next instant the exhausted man saw the current seize her and start dragging her downstream toward a foaming ladder of fang-like rapids.

Recklessly he plunged into deep water. Like most range riders, he had an instinctive dread of water and he was a poor swimmer, further handicapped by the dragging weight of his bullhide chaps and gun harness.

The current, swifter than he anticipated, seized him and bore him down on Randie. Fully conscious now, she was fighting the water like someone in the grip of a nightmare.

They were both caught in a funneling millrace and sucked into a narrow channel between moss-dappled rocks. Running the chutes of the rapids, they were carried downstream, away from the heated air of the upper canyon.

The river spread out below the rapids, only inches deep where the Gunsight Wash trail crossed it not a hundred yards around the bend beyond. Tuck floundered over to

Randie, who was standing hip-deep in the roiling green water.

Smooth rock bottom came under their boots. He saw Randie's lips moving as she recognized him, but she made no protest as he hoisted her over his shoulder and slogged over to the near bank. Both of them fell, spent and gasping, on a mattress of tules.

After the furnace heat they had just endured, the drenching spray was a blessing and a relief. They lay side by side, pulling sweet moist air into their lungs, oblivious of the smart of blistered cheeks, the acrid odor of singed hair where wind-borne sparks had struck their heads.

Finally Randie stirred and sat up like a person coming out of nightmare. Suddenly she was in Tuck's arms——

"I love you, Randie," Tuck choked out as they broke apart. "I've always loved you and wanted you—and I don't mean like a brother. I want you for my wife, Randie."

She was in his arms again. "Yes, Tuck," she breathed. "It's always been this way, I guess——"

"Do you think your father would still hold you to that promise not to marry before your birthday?"

"Cloyd was the one he didn't want me to marry. It was Cloyd who left me under that horse," she went on in a low voice. "But it was Kyle Kruze who shot the horse. It was Kruze who ordered Cloyd to set that fire."

Tuck struggled to his feet, trying to make sense out of what she had said. "Luck was with you, Randie. If you hadn't fallen on a cushion of brush you'd have had a broken leg."

They crawled up under the overhang of the dry bank together and when Randie slumped down and closed her eyes, Tuck Clayburn knew rest was her greatest need and that they would be safe here, even if the fire came down-canyon.

Gradually, as his mind cleared, Clayburn grew aware of what this fire meant to Broken Key. He got to his feet, stumbling off through the dank willow brake and cedar bosques to look up-canyon toward the fire. Smoke blotted out any view ahead.

He was turning back to rejoin Randie when he saw a dark, sodden object run the chute of the rapids and float out into this back-eddy pond. It was a dead man, face down in the water, arms and legs outspread.

That corpse had floated down-river. It could be the body of some prospector, perhaps, who had plunged into the Anviliron to escape being roasted alive, only to die by drowning.

The current was dragging the body downstream toward the tules at the mouth of Gunsight Wash. Clayburn waded into the pool, the water rising over his knees and up to his hips.

The dead man's grotesque shape was wheeling slowly in the surge of the current, his coal-black hair afloat on the ash-littered surface of the river. As Tuck reached out to seize the man's coat, he saw the slow seep of fresh blood staining the black garment, saw the round hole a bullet had made between the shoulders.

And then he saw the smoke-filtered sunlight flash on something bright on the little finger of the corpse's left hand, and he recognized the diamond ring which Randie had given back to Cloyd Weber.

"So Kyle paid you off with a bullet in the back," Tuck

175

Clayburn whispered. "You could have expected that, Weber."

He had to get Weber's corpse out of sight before Randie discovered it. He got a grip on the lawyer's sodden coat and towed his burden over to the north bank, dragged it up into the talus boulders and left it hidden behind a hedge of creosote.

Later on he would see the lawyer decently buried at this spot. Right now, he had to get back to the girl.

He was wading back across the stream when he heard a shout from down-canyon and saw Ben Tweedy, Flapjack Farley and young Chip Wayne riding toward him through the blue haze, leading his empty-saddled horse.

chapter 15

Sundown's ruddy glow, filtering blood-red through the pall of smoke which blanketed the west slope of the Furnaces, cast an unreal glare over the Broken Key trail camp where Tuck Clayburn had summoned the crew.

Except for two riders posted a mile down-canyon to keep the R Bar L steers from drifting, Broken Key's entire complement was here: grouped around Flapjack Farley's cookfire, squatting on the tongue of the chuckwagon and leaning against the hoodlum wagon.

The fire had spent itself by mid-afternoon, running out of fuel above timber line, but the glow of the charred jack pines lit the darkening sky and the smoke umbrella shut out the light of the first stars, its acrid odor pervading everything.

All things considered, luck had been with Broken Key today. The proximity of water and ample grass had kept Randie's cattle herd easy to manage; a forced draft of wind rushing up-canyon toward the conflagration had carried the scent of smoke away from the animals.

Tweedy had simply brought the drive to a halt. There were no side canyons along this stretch of the trail where stragglers could disappear. The Anviliron shallowed out, its waters presenting no danger to the cattle lining its south bank.

But the crew had eaten supper tonight in dead silence. With Clayburn and Randie Locke safely returned to their midst, there were no human casualties to grieve, no empty saddles. But the temper of Clayburn's men was ugly. This morning, a certain sense of sporting rivalry had existed in these Broken Key drovers as they contemplated the home-stretch of their trail race with Frank Jessup and his crew on the other side of Alkali Ridge. The news Tweedy had brought back concerning the hold-over of Rafter J stock at Emigrants' Meadows had given Clayburn's men fresh hope, a new lease on life. This morning, the odds had been leveling off; there was an outside chance, however slim, that Broken Key's point riders might reach the Pass ahead of Jessup's outfit.

The fire had changed all that. The riders who went up-canyon to look over the situation knew that South Canyon was barred to cattle not only today, but for weeks to come. With no rains in prospect, the jack pine snags would smoulder indefinitely. And nothing would booger a steer on the trail quicker than the sight of fire or the scent of nearby smoke.

Randie had succeeded in convincing Clayburn and old Farley that she had suffered no broken bones or severe sprains as a result of having her slain palomino fall across her leg. Bruised flesh would cause her to limp for weeks to come, but there was no necessity for loading her in a wagon and taking her back to Wagonspoke and a check-up by Doc Ashton.

None of the men spoke to the girl. They had learned of her broken engagement to Cloyd Weber—the Missourian had never been popular with any of her crew—at the same time that Clayburn had told them about Weber's setting the canyon aflame and his subsequent murder, undoubtedly at Kyle Kruze's hands.

The men knew that although Randie was not mourning Weber's death, it had been a profound shock and she was in no mood for her usual banter.

The reason behind the atmosphere of tension around the supper fire this evening was the remark Tuck Clayburn had made an hour ago, just before saddling up and heading alone, up-canyon, to attend to Cloyd Weber's burial.

"We've got three days to make our drive to Highgrade yet and we're not going to waste them," he had told his assembled riders. "But it is not going to be a matter of racing Kruze's Rafter J beef. We're going to settle that business in our own way—as soon as I get back tonight."

Not even Tweedy and Farley, Clayburn's chief lieutenants, knew what their ramrod was hinting at. All afternoon, Clayburn had remained withdrawn, unapproachable, absorbed with Broken Key's next move.

Now the crew, after an early supper, sat in a tense atmosphere of expectancy, waiting for their herd boss to come back from his grave-digging chore.

Flapjack Farley, perched as a lookout on the seat of his chuckwagon, broke the almost intolerable silence.

"Tuck's comin'. I got a hunch what is brewin,' boys. I got a hunch Tuck has got a belly full of bein' on the receivin' end of Kruze's war. I got a hunch we're goin' to hit back—and pronto."

179

Randie rose to her feet, her face grim in the dusk as she watched Tuck Clayburn ride in, dismount, and turn his horse out to graze.

The ramrod's bearded face showed the strain of this day's hellish experience. Walking in through the smoke-haze, he sized up the assembled drovers as if taking a tally. He was carrying the shovel Farley used for covering his garbage dumps at field camps. That tool had buried Cloyd Weber tonight, spelling finish to a brilliant career.

Clayburn came to a halt alongside Farley's cookfire. He said nothing, squatting on his boot heels, the curved stocks of his twin six-guns arching back from his thighs. Every eye watched him, saw the studied deliberation with which he poured himself a cup of coffee from the soot-blackened pot and returned it to simmer on the coals.

After he had finished the black brew, Clayburn tossed the tin cup into the wreckpan.

Then he began to speak. He gave the impression that he had been wrestling with a grave decision all day and that what he had to propose was distasteful in the extreme.

"Men," he said in a tone of great weariness, "tonight I am going to ask you all to join me in an act outside the sanction of the law. Up to now, Kyle Kruze has held the whip hand over Broken Key. I have had my fill of it. We are going to strike back."

If Clayburn's voice had been bugle-sharp, it could not have stirred the blood of his listeners more. This was a field general ordering attack after a long defensive campaign.

"Kruze has covered his tracks, legally, from the start," Clayburn went on. "I know he sent Trig McCoy out to the

180

potholes to ambush me as soon as he found out I was the heir to Fred's ranch, but I can't prove it.

"We know Kruze was back of the Summer Range stampede, where we lost four men and saw two of our crew hospitalized for the summer. Once again, we can't prove it in any court of law. We can't even prove this morning's forest fire was Kruze's idea."

Clayburn was speaking slowly, deliberately. He was reviewing the background of tragedy and double-dealing which had led to this morning's holocaust in South Canyon, telling his men facts they already knew, but building them up to receive whatever proposition he had formulated during the long waiting hours of this day.

"Randie knows, from what Weber told her this morning, that Kruze would have sicked his gunhawks on us today in a deliberate effort to wipe us out. But the testimony of a dead man would get us nowhere in a court of law; Kruze would only deny such a plan. We cannot even prove to a court's satisfaction that Weber was shot in the back by the renegade he worked for."

Clayburn's eyes ranged around his men, searching each face in turn, measuring them for what lay ahead.

"In other words, Kruze still holds the aces so far as taking over Broken Key later this week is concerned. The one thing we can do, the one thing we are going to do, is forestall that possibility by cleaning up Locke's debts in full, on or before high noon of July tenth."

Old Ben Tweedy said in a frustrated voice, "You don't have to sell us nothin', boss. Come to the p'int."

Clayburn grinned without mirth.

"What I am leading up to," he said, "is that I have

181

never yet advocated taking the law into our own hands. But tonight, providing you boys are willing to step outside the law in following me, we are going to fight fire with fire—we are going to buck Kyle Kruze with his own weapons."

A rumble of voices circled the tense group of Broken Key punchers, reminding Randie of dogs straining at their leashes.

"I say it is high time you got around to this meetin', Tuck," Chip Wayne grumbled. "We should o' done this the night o' the stampede."

It was Randie Locke, whose mind always ran ahead to practical things, who came to the crux of the matter.

"You mean we are going to attack Rafter J tonight, Tuck?"

Clayburn nodded. "We is not quite the word, Randie, but that is what the idea is. Scatter Jessup's beef from here to next Thursday—make it impossible for him to put a herd on the trail tomorrow. But you and Flappie won't be riding with us."

Excitement was an electric current flowing around the circle of men, their fighting instincts ignited by Clayburn's words. It remained for their straw boss, Ben Tweedy, to come up with his usual pessimistic rebuttal.

"Wait a minute, Tuck," the old man broke through the babble of voices. "Don't forget we're stuck in this canyon and will have to back-track in order to git to the other side. That will take a week or more. And our deadline is just around the corner. Scatterin' Kruze's herd won't accomplish anything. Kruze would still foreclose on us."

Tuck waited for the murmuring voices to subside.

"I've figured it this way," he said. "Gunsight Wash is

182

large enough for us to haze the herd through it and reach the Borax Road. Once we get the herd on the road, we've got a beeline in to Highgrade. But we don't want to have Rafter J to worry about. That's why we're riding over to Emigrants' Meadows tonight—to give Kruze a taste of his own medicine."

To a man, Broken Key's crew came to their feet, crowding around their range boss.

"Remember, men!" Clayburn warned them. "This little raid will put us on the wrong side of the law. Sheriff Algar could put a bounty on every one of our scalps."

The men shouted him down. There was no mistaking their temper. These riders had forgotten their fatigue, their long nights with inadequate sleep. Now their blood was fired and their appetites for violence stimulated by the prospect of tangible revenge against the author of their troubles.

"What are we waitin' fer?" Tweedy was yelling. "Let's saddle an' ride!"

Clayburn climbed up on the chuckwagon and waited for the hubbub to simmer down.

"One thing before we saddle up," he said. "I want you to remember that Kruze's drovers over at the Meadows are neighbors of ours from Frank Jessup's outfit. They no longer control Rafter J. They are probably getting Kruze's wages for this trail drive. I don't want any of Jessup's men cut down tonight unless they turn their guns on us—which they will not do."

Flapjack Farley laughed and spat on his hands.

"I'm just hopin' we tangle with Kruze and his hard cases over the ridge tonight," he said fervently. "This showdown is long overdue. We'll be doin' this for the boys who

183

died without a chance that night of the raid on Summer Range."

Within minutes Broken Key had saddled up. Every war bag yielded an extra box of ammunition. Every belt carried at least one six-shooter. Most of the punchers carried rifles in their saddle scabbards. They had started this trail drive expecting to have to defend themselves, and now their preparedness was being directed to attack instead.

Tuck Clayburn, his own blood fired by the zest of the fight this night held in prospect, spurred his steeldust stallion over to where Randie Locke was talking to Flapjack. Because of his age and poor night vision, the cook had been denied any part of this junket over the ridge tonight, an order which brought the old man close to apoplexy with rage.

"Randie," Tuck said hoarsely, "I haven't asked your opinions about this thing. I want to know this go-round has your blessing."

A bright moon had swung over the Furnace divide. Under its gleam, Tuck had never seen the girl look more hauntingly beautiful than now.

"You have my prayers tonight, Tuck. You know I love you above all else and that all I want is your safe return."

Clayburn wheeled the steeldust around, emotion constricting his throat. It was possible, he knew, that he might not live to return to her arms tonight. Her declaration of love and her benediction gave him an odd sense of comfort.

He spurred over to where his heavily-armed crew were waiting beside the river, gesturing with his arm like a cavalry commander signaling a charge.

184

The fifteen-odd riders hit the shallow ford in a body, splashing across to the far bank and up the canyon away from the herd.

They reached the side exit of Gunsight Wash and single-filed up its steep slot. A night wind was clearing the smoke out of the sky when they topped the ridge and crossed the Borax Road.

The Broken Key punchers used their mounts' breather period to check their guns, suspense mounting in them. Clayburn took this opportunity to repeat his earlier warning.

"Remember, our quarrel isn't with Frank Jessup's boys. They're not fighting us. But Kruze will most likely have his rough bunch at the Meadows. They're our meat. Let's ride."

Clayburn put his steeldust down the far slope, the Broken Key column following him in a long file. There was a good chance that Kruze might be anticipating such a raid and might have a sentinel posted on the rim of North Canyon.

They dipped down into the gorge and crossed the shallow trickle of the Anviliron's North fork. They reined upgrade at once, climbing the far wall of the canyon and fanning out when they reached the upper ridge.

Below them, Emigrants' Meadows lay under the moon, the bedded-down herd plainly visible even from this distance. The glow of Jessup's campfire was a blinking spark down at the edge of the springs.

Clayburn held up his arm, halting the men. This was to be the battleground. They spotted the white gleam of Jessup's canvas-hooded chuckwagon, proving that the campfire was no dummy to draw them away from the location of the Rafter J camp.

The night was still. Nothing disturbed the tranquility of the grassy bench. The rarefied air here at the eight-thousand-foot level brought to their ears the faint crooning of Jessup's nighthawks circling the bedground.

Clayburn's senses were tuned to a high pitch of perceptivity. He had not expected this quiet reception; surely Kruze's riders had been forewarned by now of this reprisal in the making.

Tuck snaked his carbine from leather and spoke in a low voice to his men, poised here on the ridge, impatient for the charge.

"We will risk riding into a trap here. I am going to signal Jessup's camp, men. I want to make sure that Rafter J knows who we are and what we're going to do. Once they know the set-up, any one of them who fires at us is on his own."

Resting the butt plate of his Winchester on his saddle pommel, Clayburn triggered a shot skyward. The crash of the report carried across the Meadows, repeated and flung back in echo by a hundred far crags and ridges.

The riders behind Clayburn reined in their horses, each animal startled into little mincing steps. From the bedground they heard a sporadic snort from nervous cattle; the sound of a circle rider cursing whoever had fired the shot.

Clayburn cradled the fuming rifle across his lap, cupped hands to mouth and sent a stentorian call toward the chuckwagon camp down by the water hole:

"Halloo, the camp! Jessup, you hear me?"

There was a momentary silence from the flats. Then a

quavering voice floated back on the night. Every man recognized old Frank Jessup. "That you up yonder, Clayburn?"

"This is Broken Key, Frank," Clayburn yelled back. "We're busting up your herd tonight. We got no quarrel with Rafter J. But we're loaded for bear and we'll shoot at anybody who shoots at us. Pass the word to your boys."

Broken Key's riders sat their saddles tautly, poised like jockeys at the start of a race. They knew that Clayburn's next move would be to signal the attack, as soon as he got Frank Jessup's confirmation of what was coming.

Black shapes crossed and recrossed the campfire down there, indicating a bustle of action at the water hole. Then Jessup's strident yell reached them:

"Broken Key—don't ride in! Kruze is running this she-bang and he's got his gunnies strung out in them rocks east of you—watch sharp they don't cut around behind yuh!"

Hard on the heels of Jessup's warning, the night erupted to a drumroll of rifle fire, bore flashes sparkling like jewels on a necklace along the rocky perimeter of the ridge.

A sleet of steel-jacketed lead whined around the Broken Key column as the men swung to meet this ambush fire.

Clayburn heard the thwack of a random slug hitting young Chip Wayne, the rider nearest his stirrup, and he heard Chip's gasp as he slumped in saddle and slid quietly to the ground.

This surprise attack from at least a dozen guns brought momentary confusion to Broken Key's ranks. It was here that Tuck Clayburn's leadership would have its test, and he rose to meet it now.

"Unhorse and belly down, boys!" Tuck yelled. "We've

187

got to charge those rocks and smoke Kyle's bunch at hand-to-hand range before we go on down to the flats."

As if in answer to Clayburn's shout, the challenging voice of Kyle Kruze himself lashed out from the nearby boulders:

"Leave Clayburn for me, boys! Tuck Clayburn's my target—so let 'em come! We're waitin' for you buzzards, Broken Key! The closer the better!"

chapter 16

THE pattern of violence took shape in the first bullet-shrieking seconds of combat; that soon did Kruze's concealed gunslingers see their advantage reach its peak and the tide of battle start swinging against them.

Frank Jessup had risked much to give Broken Key its warning. Otherwise Kruze would have sprung his death-trap only after Clayburn had led his crew down the ridge into a situation menaced by total destruction from above and behind.

But Jessup had touched off the ambush fire prematurely, giving Clayburn's invading crew their chance to dive from saddle and thus reduce the target advantage to nearly zero.

Clayburn and his Broken Key guns scuttled across the ground, their milling horses adding to the confusion with their kicked-up dusk and moving shapes. They had reversed the predictable by charging instead of withdrawing to shelter from which they could make a protracted shoot-out of this thing.

The latter course was the safer, but it would have meant the pitched battle would have shortly become a stalemate which would have lasted out the night without settling the issue.

As it was, Clayburn's reckless strategy confronted Kruze's paid gunhawks with the unpleasant prospect of a hand-to-hand showdown with gun and knife and knuckle.

Broken Key's first desperate rush under the screen of dust carried them into the jumble of glacial boulders. They timed their rushes between salvos from the hidden ambushers.

A counter volley from Broken Key sent bullets screaming and ricocheting through the tangle of rocks, further confusing Kruze's professional gunfighters.

Shouting like red savages, Clayburn and his revenge-hungry crew poured among the rocks in a fanned-out skirmish line, firing at every darting shadow or silhouetted target ahead of them.

In the face of that determined and unforeseen charge, Kruze's faction lost its nerve and with it any chance of standing off Broken Key's assault.

Close infighting, against slightly superior numerical odds, went against the grain of the mercenaries Kruze had recruited from his saloons in Wagonspoke. They preferred to work with the odds in their favor, as they had at Summer Range. Theirs was the tradition of the knife in the back, the shot from ambush, the club in a dark alley.

Clayburn, leading his fast charge through the litter of boulders, heard the opposing gunfire taper off, heard Kyle Kruze's infuriated cursing farther along the brow of the hill as he tried to rally his retreating forces.

Broken Key's drovers, sensing the swing of battle was in their favor now, renewed their shouts and took to vaulting rocks instead of skulking around them.

Reaching the brow of the rocky divide they were storming, they caught sight of Kyle Kruze's defenders in wild rout on foot, sprinting toward the shadowy refuge of North Canyon.

Broken Key gunmen holstered their hot-barreled six-shooters and used their rifles to pour a violent fire at the retreating enemy. It was tricky shooting, at long range and in obscure moonlight, but they saw man after man go down before the last of them vanished into the canyon's fastnesses.

Clayburn, knowing that Kruze's faction had been decisively knocked out of the fight, made no attempt to hold back the murderous fire of his crew. That would have been as impossible as restraining a wolf pack that had tasted blood. They had the Summer Range massacre to avenge; probably this would be their last chance to come to grips with Kruze's owlhoot crew.

Shouting "Take over, Ben!" to his grizzled roustabout, Tuck Clayburn made his way back over the rock-littered ridge and came out on the lower slope overlooking Jessup's camp. He recognized his steeldust gelding among the loose ponies about him, caught up with it and mounted.

The gunfire over the ridge toward North Canyon was silent now, as Broken Key found no more targets visible. Clayburn, riding straight toward Jessup's camp, sent his identifying shout on ahead of him. He had to be sure Kruze hadn't planted men with Jessup's crew.

"It's OK—come on down, Tuck!" Jessup called out, walking away from his water hole camp. "You got my word no man of mine will draw cards in a ruckus with Broken Key. You been my neighbors too long for that."

191

Meeting the white-haired Rafter J boss, Clayburn dismounted.

"I don't like what I'm going to have to do to your cattle tonight," he greeted Jessup over a handshake.

Jessup shrugged. "They ain't my cattle, son. Kruze took over my ranch a week ago. He offered me and my boys a hundred dollars apiece for the ten-day job of hazin' my beef up to Highgrade. I took the proposition, not knowin' at the time you had a herd on the trail too."

Clayburn said gently, "I know, Frank."

Jessup said, "You tally Kruze?"

"I won't know until the boys have had time to look over our bag. We got our share of meat, I know that, up in the rocks and on the slope leading down to the canyon rim."

Jessup's rheumy eyes held a tragic shine as he peered at his neighbor.

"When Kruze planted his saloon toughs in them rocks, I had a hunch you was goin' to come over the ridge and jump us tonight, son. I warned my boys if shootin' started, they was to take no part in it."

Clayburn laughed. "Thanks for tipping me off to Kruze's trap, old timer. Now, as soon as the boys round up their nags, we're going to scatter this herd from hell to breakfast."

Jessup said, "Is that necessary now, son, with Kruze on the run?"

"Kruze was within the law, hiring men to defend his herd from rustlers tonight. We raided him, not vice versa. He could still come back tomorrow and order you to put your cattle on the trail."

Jessup thought that over and saw the logic behind the

grim necessity back of the scattering of his herd. It would take weeks to round them up out of these Furnace canyons and draws. Having lost his ranch, Jessup would abandon these cattle bearing his iron. Recovering them was Kruze's responsibility.

"Like I say, I didn't know until yesterday that us winnin' this trail race meant Broken Key's finish," Jessup said. "Tell you what. My boys will help you scatter the herd tonight. We're both fightin' the same range hog, I reckon. If Broken Key survives, I'm li'ble to be askin' you for a ridin' job."

Rafter J punchers were beginning to drift out from their camp now, halting at a respectful distance. On the Meadow flats the herd was restless, poised to stampede by the recent gunfire on the ridge. Scattering them would be simple, much as it might go against the grain of the drovers.

"That will be a big favor, Frank," Clayburn said. "It goes without saying Kruze won't pay off for the work you've done getting the herd this far. Tell your boys if Broken Key comes out of this thing intact, we will make good the wages Kruze promised them."

Tuck remounted and put his horse back up the slope. By the time he had reached the motionless sprawl at the summit which was Chip Wayne's corpse, cut down in the opening moments of the melee, his crew was beginning to drift back with battle reports.

Down at the water hole camp, Jessup had his men saddling up with orders to help scatter Kruze's beef so thoroughly that the Wagonspoke gambler would find it

193

impossible to hire a crew to gather them and put them back on the Highgrade trail again.

Singly and by twos and threes, the Broken Key boys came back from the chase. Counting noses, Clayburn was infinitely relieved to learn that young Wayne was their only casualty.

"We tallied eight of the devil's dozen," Ben Tweedy reported. The roustabout had a crimson smear across one cheek, which he swore was a ricochet from behind, a bullet fired from a Broken Key gun. "There were only four others who high-tailed it into the canyon."

Clayburn said harshly, "Kruze was one of them?"

"Afraid so, kid. Leastwise I think that was his voice I heard yellin' in the canyon. They had hosses stashed down there, I know that."

By the time Broken Key had recovered their scattered horses, strays quickly rounded up by the ropes of the men with mounts, Frank Jessup's crew was at work stampeding Kruze's cattle out of the Meadows. By morning this grazing area would be empty of Rafter J beef.

Clayburn personally attended to the sad chore of lashing Chip Wayne's body to his saddle. Every man realized they were lucky there were not more graves to dig tomorrow.

On their trek back to rejoin Randie and Flapjack in South Canyon, Ben Tweedy voiced the question which was in every Broken Key mind:

"Well, boss, where do we stand now? Looks to me like we got better than an even chance to collect on Garbie's contract to take our herd before the tenth."

Clayburn took a long time about answering that one.

Total victory was not entirely in their grasp yet, despite the success of tonight's bloody foray against Kruze.

"It depends," he said, "on what luck we have hazing the stock through Gunsight Wash and up the Borax Road to the Pass. This is the eighth, ain't it? Two days. It will be shaving it mighty thin."

Tweedy said boastfully, "We'll do 'er, kid. For Randie's sake as well as Broken Key's. We'll do 'er."

One of the punchers spoke up wearily, "Thing that bothers me, Tuck, is getting that *dinero* back to the bank in time. Say we collect from Mose Kaploon on the tenth. Yore deadline at Moon's bank is noon that day, ain't it? How's a man going to get back to Wagonspoke, damn nigh eighty miles, in time?"

Clayburn laughed. "We're not collecting our money from Kaploon, Shorty. Only a receipt for the delivered herd."

"Then how——"

"The telegraph, Shorty. We'll telegraph Garbie, or have Kaploon do it. Garbie will deposit a hundred thousand to Broken Key's account. You can depend on Clem Moon tearin' up those foreclosure papers for us before Kruze gets a chance to call for 'em."

Chip Wayne's body was put on the hoodlum wagon and started back to Verde Valley for burial in Wagonspoke's boothill cemetery at dawn the following day.

And then Tuck and his crew, without benefit of a night's rest, got their Broken Key herd on the trail again. From now on, time was their only enemy; the backbone of Kyle Kruze's resistance had been crushed by last night's foray at Emigrants' Meadows.

195

In the end, it was the help of Frank Jessup and his ten Rafter J cowpokes which turned the trick in their favor. Augmented by their neighbors at mid-morning, the drovers encountered little difficulty in shunting the herd out of South Canyon's channel and into the side exit of Gunsight Wash.

They had the entire herd strung out on the Borax Road by nightfall.

Dawn of July ninth found the combined crews in saddle and the herd, bunched compactly and too hoof-sore to stampede, reached the confluence of the two branches of Anviliron at high noon.

Seeing the brown flood of bawling animals funneling into the narrow slot of Wagongap Pass, Randie Locke and Tuck Clayburn knew the long gamble had paid off. From here on to Garbie's holding ground at Wildrose Flats was a level road which they could cover, without crowding the animals, by the middle of tomorrow morning.

Notifying Garbie down in Wagonspoke of the successful meeting of the contract deadline would require but a matter of minutes, through the magic of the Overland Telegraph. For the first time since he had ordered the round-up of Randie's beef in Broken Key's Summer Range, Tuck Clayburn felt he could breathe easy again.

He rode up the Pass ahead of the herd with Randie at his side. Nightfall found the Broken Key herd bedded down at the old Wells Fargo station.

A scant three miles separated them from Garbie's pasture at Wildrose now. With Frank Jessup's crew to assist in the driving, this last short leg of the drive was as good as won.

July tenth's fateful sunrise found the herd under way again, for Clayburn was taking no chances on last-minute delays. Not until they reached the turnoff to Highgrade and Ben Tweedy had been shown the bedground at Wildrose did Clayburn relax his vigilance.

"You're riding to Highgrade with me, Randie," he told the girl at his side. "It's quite a sight, a gold camp at the peak of its excitement. Do you know what I aim to do, as soon as Kaploon has put that telegram on the wires to Garbie?"

The girl cocked her head and regarded him saucily.

"I can't imagine, Tuck," she laughed. "Get shaved, I hope. You're as shaggy as a gorilla."

Clayburn rubbed the wiry, two weeks' growth of stubble furring his lean jaw. A vagrant thought crossed his mind: a sign he had seen outside a ramshackle tent-house in camp, offering the use of a zinc bathtub and twenty gallons of water for five dollars—"Bring Yore Own Soap & Towel." Right now, he would have given a month's wages for a bath.

"I'm going to scour Highgrade from one end to the other," he told the girl, "huntin' up a sky pilot. So when we ride back to Broken Key it will be as man and wife."

The girl reined over close beside him, her face tender, her eyes wistful. They leaned from saddle, oblivious to all else around them, and it took the jeering remarks of a passing prospector to break them out of their embrace, long minutes later.

"I can see only one objection to getting married up here, and I'll leave that to you, sweetheart," Randie said as they resumed their ride. "Doc Ashton always wanted to see me take my vows, he's told me a thousand times. He brought me into the world. He said there were two other things he wanted to do before he died—see me safely married off be-

197

fore I turned into an old maid—and deliver my first baby."

Clayburn grinned, his eyes on the first glimpse of High-grade's panorama as they rounded a point of high ground. Their ears picked up the shuddering reverberations of the stampmill which marked the pulse beat of this gold camp's resurrection.

"Aw, we prob'ly won't find a preacher in this hell-hole anyway," he said, "so Ashton will get his wish."

A mile behind them, Ben Tweedy's yipping drovers were pushing the Broken Key herd onto Garbie's graze. The long ordeal was over, its hazards run; only the pay-off remained to be consummated.

Randie Locke consulted her mother's watch, which she habitually carried in the pocket of her levis. Kruze's deadline was two hours and twenty minutes away, at the Cattlemen's Bank in Wagonspoke.

"It has been a close thing, my darling," she said to the man who rode tall in the saddle beside her. "A hairline finish. But we have won."

Tuck Clayburn nodded, his eyes fixed on the false front of Mose Kaploon's mercantile, which was their destination. He shared the girl's gladness, the feeling that their climactic hour was behind them.

But this fight would not be won until Gabe Garbie delivered a hundred thousand dollars in gold to Clem Moon's bank, upon receipt of Kaploon's telegraphic confirmation that the R Bar L herd had met its contractual deadline this morning.

A game was never over until the turn of the last card, and the last card in this drama had yet to be played. Not until it was would Tuck Clayburn take victory for granted.

chapter 17

KYLE KRUZE and Mose Kaploon faced each other in the dingy half-light of the storekeeper's boxed-off sleeping quarters in the rear of Highgrade's mercantile store.

The gold slugs made a chinking little tune as the Wagonspoke gambler built up the little stacks of coin like a card player shoving chips into a high stakes pot.

"It's not like you were cutting yourself out of a profit on that beef, Mose," Kruze explained. "All I'm asking you to do is delay purchase of those cattle until this afternoon. Then you can pay Randie Locke her price."

Kaploon ran a finger around the inside of his collar band, sweat flowing from his caved-in cheeks like beadlets of wax.

"Thing is, Kruze, the boss down in Wagonspoke made his deal with Clayburn out o' his regard for Fred Locke's memory."

Kruze laughed scornfully. "You mean Gabe Garbie saw a chance to cash in big, selling beefsteaks to miners at the highest prices in history," the gambler said. "If you're thinking about Randie, if you're squeamish about buckin' a woman—let me point out that her and Clayburn probably will get married right away and they'll have a hundred thousand of Garbie's money for a wedding present. You won't be hurting anybody but yourself if you turn down this offer."

Kaploon stared at the yellow metal stacked on his deal table with the yearning of a man who had worked hard all his life for other men. Kruze had counted out ten thousand in gold which would be Kaploon's for the asking. He could live like a king for ten thousand dollars—revel in luxury for the rest of his life.

"Let me ask you something," Kyle Kruze went on persuasively. "How much salary does Garbie pay you for slaving around the clock at this store?"

"Fifty a month and my groceries an' duds."

"Fifty a month! And who'll get a thousand percent profit you'll make selling fresh meat to these jackleg muckers? Not you, Mose. You'll ship your profits back to Wagonspoke, to be deposited in Gabe Garbie's name. Don't be a sucker. You're not cheating Garbie, holding up payment on that beef."

Kaploon whispered craftily, "You don't have to draw a picture for me, Kyle. You got a million-dollar cattle ranch that'll be yores in another couple hours, if Clayburn don't telegraph Wagonspoke that I've taken delivery on his herd."

Kruze tilted back his chair, his eyes flashing.

"I'm offering you ten thousand to save myself a ranch that'll be worth a million in a few years," Kruze admitted. "It's a business proposition and nothing else, Mose."

200

Kaploon tore his eyes off the stacked octagonals and met the gambler's level gaze.

"Make this bribe twenty thousand, Kyle, and——"

Kruze came to his feet, anger darkening his cheeks. He whipped open the flap of the cantle pouch he had carried the gold in and reached over the table, sweeping the stacked specie into a heap.

"You can go to hell, Mose. I'm not raising my ante."

Kaploon bounced out of his chair, reaching out to seize the gambler's wrist before he could begin scooping the gold slugs back into his saddlebag.

"Don't, Kruze. You—you win. I'll stall Clayburn off when he gits here."

Kruze shook off the storekeeper's grip and began counting off coins in two-hundred-dollar stacks.

"Your little attempt to gouge me," Kruze said, "is going to cost you five thousand, Kaploon. And you'll take my offer and like it, you sniveling little wart hog."

Kruze had measured his man's price correctly. When he left the office five minutes later, Mose Kaploon was scooping his five-thousand-dollar prize into a carpetbag, cursing his own greed with a bitter vehemence.

"Ort to have my tongue cut out," he groaned. "Wagged it onct too often an' it cost me ten years' wages."

Kaploon was in the front of his store, haggling with a miner over the price of a red shirt, when he caught sight of Tuck Clayburn and Randie Locke reining up in front of his mercantile.

He hastily concluded his sale with the miner and was alone in the store when the two Broken Key riders came in.

"Well, Mose," Clayburn sang out cheerfully, "the herd's at Wildrose. We made it."

Kaploon shook hands with Clayburn and the girl, his voice noncommittal as he asked, "What's the tally, so I'll know what to telegraph Gabe?"

Clayburn said off-handedly, "Call it an even five hundred. It'll run ten-twenty head over that figure, but we'll throw that in as a bonus."

When Kaploon made no answer, Randie Locke checked her watch with the fly-speckled clock on the store wall and said anxiously, "It's ten-fifteen, Mr. Kaploon. Put us out of our misery and write out that telegram. We'll take it to the office and get it on the wire."

Kaploon fingered his beard nervously.

"Hold on, now," he said evasively. "This here is a business proposition. I got to play this practical."

Alarm glimmered in Clayburn's eyes. He knew that Kaploon was a hard-fisted skinflint when it came to business matters, at least as penurious as his shrewd boss in Wagonspoke.

"What do you mean, practical?" the Broken Key ramrod demanded. "Aren't you taking my word for the tally?"

Kaploon shrugged. "More'n that, son. I heard about that fire wipin' out yore South Canyon 'tother day. Last I heard, yore cows were bunched up at dead end."

Randie said desperately, "But we drove them up the ridge and into the Pass by way of the Borax Road. They're out at your holding ground right this minute, Mr. Kaploon. You have no reason at all for stalling us."

Kaploon held up a palsied hand.

"Now, now, Miss Locke, don't fergit we ain't playin'

202

penny-ante here. This deal goes into six figgers. I can't authorize nothin' that steep without goin' out to Wildrose an' seein' that herd with my own eyes."

Clayburn and Randie exchanged dumfounded stares. They had not anticipated this stubborn streak of Kaploon's.

"You mean—you want to count 'em?" Clayburn demanded in a stricken voice. "Can't you take my word for the tally—for the fact the herd has been delivered?"

Kaploon hobbled his way toward the front of the store, his jaw clamped adamantly. He reached for a battered straw hat hanging from a wall peg and clapped it on his bald head, then turned to face the anxious pair.

"Business," the old trader said stubbornly, "is business. If it's that telegram yo're worryin' about, forget it. I won't insist on a tally, not after I've sized up the herd myself. I can make it out to Wildrose an' back easy by eleven-thirty."

Clayburn and the girl followed Kaploon down the length of the store and out the back door, the storeman heading for his lean-to stable where he kept a strawberry roan mare.

Desperation was in Clayburn as he argued, "That's shaving it too fine, Mose. What in hell has come over you, getting technical this way? You know what this means to Randie and me—it means losing Broken Key if your horse throws a shoe and goes lame on you——"

Kaploon went about saddling the roan with a studied air of aloofness. Clayburn saw now that there would be no breaking this trader's will.

"I'm not a-tryin' to throw a monkey wrench into yore plans, Clayburn," Mose Kaploon said reassuringly. "Ifn you was in my place you'd check the bet yoreself. It ain't my money I'm dealin' with, it's Gabe's. I ain't run Gabe's store for him all these years by takin' other men's word for anything, and I ain't a-goin' to change my ways now."

As they watched the old man climb clumsily into stirrups, Randie said imploringly, "You'll hurry back, won't you? So much is at stake——"

Kaploon grinned. "For you, Miss Locke, I'll run this nag's hoofs down to the frawgs. Now don't you worry about a thing, understand?"

With a sick sense of time fast running out on them, Clayburn and Randie saw Kaploon head at a jog trot up the alley flanking his store, to vanish from view in the main street's traffic.

"He *will* make it back in time to send that wire, won't he, Tuck?" Randie said in a weak voice.

Anger put its raw fixture on Clayburn's face as they turned back into the deserted store.

"He will if his horse don't fall dead on him," Tuck said. "He can make it back in an hour, if he doesn't stop to chew the rag with Ben Tweedy and the boys. I think to play it safe I'd better leave you here and ride out to Wildrose with Kaploon, Randie."

They were threading their way through Kaploon's cluttered store when they caught sight of the tall, silhouetted figure outlined against the street windows. A customer had come in during their absence and was fishing tools out of a box of miscellaneous merchandise.

"How much you asking for these wire pinchers, Mose?" a voice greeted them as they were passing the huge pot-belly stove mid-way up the store's length.

Clayburn came to a halt, pushing out his arm to stop Randie.

The man who was examining the big wire cutters up by the front window was Kyle Kruze.

"Kaploon," Clayburn said in a biting voice, "has stepped out of the store, Kruze."

Clayburn was loosening his six-guns in holsters as he headed on up the aisle toward the Wagonspoke gambler. He had not heard Kruze's slurring voice since the other night at Emigrants' Meadows when the big man had shouted to his ambushed crew to leave Clayburn for his own personal target.

Now they were face to face, and Clayburn's blood was on fire with a riotous urge to pick up their fight where they had left off with Kruze's flight.

Kruze swung around to face Clayburn in the dim light of the store, one hand holding the massive wire cutters like a club, the other swinging loose at his side.

Kruze was wearing his black fustian coat, the tails of which concealed the big stocks of his own guns. Clayburn knew of the gambler's habit of carrying .41 derringers under his sleeve cuffs and he was on guard now for any slight twitch of a wrist which might telegraph Kruze's intention of using the hide-out pistols.

Instead, Kruze kept his arms hanging at his sides, a taut smile showing his gold-capped teeth under the thin black line of his mustache.

"I want to congratulate you, Tuck," Kruze said in a smooth monotone. "I saw your herd leaving the Pass this morning. I assume that by now the good news is on its way to Wagonspoke. Fred Locke knew what he was doing when he put the destiny of Broken Key in your hands."

Behind Clayburn's crouched figure, Randie Locke was

moving toward a nearby counter, knowing that gunplay might break out of this explosive meeting at any second. She coughed loudly to signal Clayburn that she had placed herself out of the line of fire.

"Kruze," Clayburn said in a controlled voice, "I am returning to Wagonspoke tomorrow. There's something you've got to know."

Kruze shrugged. "I'll be heading back home myself, Clayburn. Perhaps we can make the trip together."

Clayburn moved in closer, every nerve and muscle primed for a gun-draw if the big gambler made the first false move.

"That's what I wanted to tell you, Kruze," the Broken Key man went on in his menace-charged voice. "The time has come when Wagonspoke can't hold the two of us. One of us has got to clear out. And it won't be me, Kruze."

Kruze's inscrutable face did not change expression by so much as a twitch of an eyelid.

"An ultimatum, Clayburn? Are you forgetting that there is no ill will between you and me, at least as far as I am concerned? Are you forgetting that I proved my own feeling toward you when I withdrew my charges after you shot McCoy?"

Knots of muscle ground at the corners of Clayburn's jaws. He was impotent before this calm avowal of friendship on Kruze's part. He was deliberately trying to bait Kruze into making a hostile move, and Kruze was laughing at him with his eyes.

"The McCoy case," Clayburn said angrily, "was a deal between you and Cloyd Weber. And Weber is dead and buried. You killed him."

Kruze's brows arched.

"I killed my own lawyer? Are those the grounds you hope to justify——"

"I'm telling you, Kruze, that if I find you in Wagonspoke I will kill you. If you think your chances of calling my bet are any better here in Highgrade, make your play."

For a long moment, Kruze thought over Clayburn's challenge without moving from his statue-still posture.

Then, very slowly, he turned his back on the threat of Clayburn's guns and walked to the door.

Pausing there to tuck the heavy wire clippers under one arm, Kruze opened the door and then turned to face the Broken Key man.

"I prefer to choose the time and the place," he said quietly, "for settling any business between us, Clayburn. Maybe the ride down to Verde Valley will cool you off. Right now you are not in your usual good mood. I would not want to have your blood on my conscience under the circumstances."

Randie Locke came up to join Tuck Clayburn as her ramrod watched Kruze descend the porch steps outside, duck under the hitching rail and untie his big grulla stallion.

The two of them emerged from the store as Kruze mounted, curvetted his horse out into the street, and then, without a backward look, spurred off in the direction of the Pass.

"Tuck," the girl whispered, "you know that man will never face you in open showdown. The minute he gets to town he'll send bushwhackers up to meet you in the foothills."

Clayburn was trembling with a sense of anticlimax, with the feeling that Kruze, and not himself, had emerged victor from this clash of wills.

"Randie," Clayburn said in a shaken voice, "I think Kruze has Mose Kaploon in his pocket. I think Kruze is back of Mose's stalling us this morning. I don't think Kaploon intends to get back from inspecting our herd—until after the bank's deadline has gone by."

Randie Locke's face went ashen. She felt Clayburn grip her savagely by the arm.

"Randie," Tuck whispered desperately, "I'm going to send that wire—over Kaploon's name. Come on."

He headed down the store's steps with strides which forced the girl to run to keep up with him.

Threading their way through the mining camp's congested street, they crossed over to the Reno-Bishop Overland Telegraph Office, only to find the door locked and a scribbled sign tacked over the knob:

OFFICE CLOSED. LEAVE MESSAGES IN SLOT. IN EMERGENCY, CALL AT THE GREEN ROOSTER AND ASK FOR CY ANDRADE.

"Wait here," Clayburn said harshly. "I've got to chase down that operator. Don't leave this spot, Randie."

Before the girl could speak Clayburn was on his way up the street, heading toward the old saloon which had been built out of empty beer bottles and adobe mortar when Highgrade had been in the throes of its first gold rush.

He found no trace of the telegrapher in the Green Rooster, but the jaded bartender told him Andrade would most likely be eating his lunch at his dugout up on the west ridge at this hour of the day.

The hands of Randie Locke's watch stood at eleven-twenty o'clock when Tuck Clayburn finally arrived at the Overland Telegraph office with Cy Andrade in tow. They had lost a precious hour tracking the Highgrade pioneer down. Clayburn eventually had found the man playing fan-tan with a group of Chinese prospectors at the Highgrade Discovery Mine's tailing dump.

After what seemed an interminable delay, the muttering oldster got his door unlocked and Clayburn and Randie crowded inside. Andrade made his way through a drop leaf behind a littered counter and sat down beside his clattering telegraph sounder.

Snatching up a pencil and paper, Clayburn scribbled his message with feverish haste:

GABRIEL GARBIE,
c/o VALLEY MERCANTILE,
WAGONSPOKE, CALIF.
    HERD DELIVERED PER CONTRACT URGENT YOU AUTHORIZE PAYMENT TO CLEM MOON AT BANK IMMEDIATELY

He signed the telegram "Moses Kaploon" and thrust it in Andrade's hand.

The old brasspounder scanned Clayburn's writing, scowled, then looked up suspiciously.

"Ag'in company rules to put a message on the wires when it bears a name other than the sender, Tuck," Andrade said officiously. "You better traipse over to the store an' fetch Kaploon in to verify this."

Sweat burst from the cowpuncher's cheeks. "Put *my* name on it, then. Kaploon's out of town. Hurry it up, Cy."

Andrade shrugged, scratched out Kaploon's name and substituted Clayburn's, and then mounted the stool beside his instrument table and threw a switch to transmitting position.

He checked his key for clearance, muttering through his beard, "Yo're lucky, son. Line's open to Wagonspoke. Sometimes the Reno office ties it up fer hours at a stretch."

Andrade's scraggy fist began translating Clayburn's message into dots and dashes. After a few seconds, the noisy sounder on its collapsible bracket at Andrade's side went dead.

That fact would have held no significance for the couple waiting beyond the telegrapher's counter had it not been for the sudden reach Andrade made for his switch, hammering at the insulated handle, than rattling his key. The sounder remained mute.

Forgetting Randie's presence in his office, Cy Andrade exploded in a sulphurous tirade of profanity which would have shamed a mulewhacker's vocabulary.

"Line's gone dead on me," he shouted, turning to face Clayburn and the girl. "Some pesky camper has chopped down a pole to use fer firewood, between here an' Wagonspoke, reckon. Or else some miner wantin' handy wood fer shorin' up a prospect hole."

Clayburn swayed, gripping the pine counter for support. "You mean—you can't get my message through?"

Andrade gave his telegraph key another touch.

"Not until I locate the break in the wire. Which same may take a day or two."

210

Clayburn turned slowly to face the girl at his side.

"Those pinchers Kyle Kruze carried out of Kaploon's store," he cawed in a throaty whisper. "Kruze used 'em to cut the telegraph wire as soon as he got out of sight of town. I was a crazy blind fool not to have known he'd do that."

Tears blinded Randie Locke. There was no time to hunt down the break and repair it. Here at the eleventh hour, Kyle Kruze had played his ace in the hole. Broken Key was lost.

chapter 18

BROKEN KEY'S homecoming was like a funeral procession. This was late afternoon of July eleventh, thirty hours after the expiration of Kyle Kruze's deadline on Fred Locke's indebtedness against the ranch. The need for haste, which had tinctured every move Clayburn had made in the past three weeks, was gone.

He and Randie were not making the ride back from the Furnaces alone. Although Rafter J's crew had remained at the gold camp to try their luck with pick and pan in Highgrade's outlying canyons, the Broken Key crew, including ex-prospector Ben Tweedy, had elected to make this last ride back to their home spread.

Ostensibly, these work-worn ranch hands were returning to Broken Key's bunkhouse to pick up their meager personal belongings before quitting the ranch forever. Some of them had spent the better part of their adult lives on Locke's payroll.

In reality, the men were making their last gesture of devotion to Randie Locke and Tuck Clayburn, escorting them back to the range they had fought for and lost.

Nature herself had turned traitor against them. To the

west, above the Sierra Nevadas, vast thunderhead cloud formations were piling up, promising Verde Valley its first summer rainstorm in nearly half a decade. This change in the weather would have been welcome at any other time, presaging as it did the inevitable end of a lengthy dry cycle.

But now, added to everything else, the prospect of rain in the Lavastones had a depressing effect upon the riders who had watched Locke's graze revert to desert over the dry years. Even the weather was turning in Kruze's favor.

Nearing the outskirts of Wagonspoke, where the road to Anvil Mesa forked off, the gloomy cavalcade reined up around Flapjack Farley's chuckwagon.

Clayburn turned to Randie, his face heavy.

"You go on out to the ranch with the boys and start packing up," he said. "This much I can promise you: Kruze may be out there when you arrive, but he won't stay long. Not after I——"

Clayburn broke off as the sound of a rider leaving town on the run reached his ears. All heads turned to see the bulky shape of Arnie Algar heading their way, his sheriff's badge gleaming dully from a gallus strap.

No word was spoken as the old sheriff rode up to the disconsolate group and reined in. Algar cocked an eye toward the ominous leaden sky to westward.

"Fixin' to rain," he remarked banally. "Thought I'd never live to see this glad day."

Receiving no answer, Algar stared at Clayburn.

"I'll have to ask for your guns, kid, unless you're by-passing the town."

Clayburn stirred in the saddle.

Algar looked embarrassed. "Kyle Kruze tells me you've

213

given him his walking papers. It's my duty to keep you two from locking horns, kid."

"Kruze is in town?"

"He's still in town," Algar acknowledged.

Ben Tweedy called out sharply, "You disarmed Kruze, sheriff? And his hard cases at the saloon?"

Algar said defensively, "Kruze is not the aggressor in this case. He hit town this morning and reported that you were huntin' him, Tuck. Either steer clear of town for the time being or hand over your irons."

Clayburn matched the sheriff's look for a long moment. Then he turned to his crew.

"Go on out to the spread," he said. "I want to talk things over with the sheriff."

The Broken Key bunch shifted uneasily in saddle. Randie, who was riding in the chuckwagon with Farley, said in a broken voice:

"Sheriff, Tuck aims to swear out a warrant for Kruze's arrest. He shot and killed Cloyd Weber. I—I am the witness who will appear in court against him."

Algar straightened in saddle, his jaw dropping.

"Kruze shot that lawyer? I hadn't heard——"

Clayburn said impatiently, "There are a lot of things you haven't heard, sheriff. Let's go."

Algar wheeled his pony around, spurring after Clayburn as the Broken Key puncher, having made no move to turn over his guns, headed toward Wagonspoke at a gallop.

Behind them, Farley's chuckwagon got into motion, leading the dejected riders down the Broken Key road.

In front of Kyle Kruze's Montalto Casino, Clayburn reined up and dismounted, the sheriff following suit rapidly.

214

The old lawman had a gun palmed as Clayburn headed toward the door of the deadfall, only to find it locked.

There was a note on the door:

AM AT THE BANK. K.K.

Clayburn said bitterly, "Making sure Clem Moon handled the foreclosure papers according to Hoyle, I reckon. Sheriff, we lost Broken Key."

Algar holstered his six-gun cautiously.

"I'm sorry to hear that, son. I—I know you figger you got provocation enough to take the law into yore own hands and clean Kruze's plow for him. But I can't let you go on the dodge, you savvy that, don't you?"

A remote mutter of thunder, west of the Lavastones, reached their ears as the two began leading their horses down the street in the direction of the Cattlemen's Bank.

"We got the herd to Highgrade ahead of the deadline," Clayburn was saying in a dead voice, "but Kruze cut the telegraph line on us. Made off with a hundred feet of wire between two poles, so it couldn't be patched up in time."

They tied their horses at the bank's railing. Clayburn peered up at the second-story windows, at the faded letters reading PAUL ASHTON, M.D. He wondered if Fred Locke's old crony had heard the bad news about Broken Key.

At the door of the bank vestibule, Arnie Algar reached out a restraining hand.

"If Kruze is in there," he said hoarsely, "he'll take one look at you and start foggin' his guns, Tuck, unless he sees you ain't heeled."

Before the aged lawman could interfere, Clayburn shook

215

off his grasp and opened the bank door. The lobby was deserted, teller's wickets closed for the day. The sheriff overtook Clayburn on his way to the door of Clem Moon's private office.

"Tuck," Algar said desperately, "don't force me to throw a gun on you. I don't like Kruze's guts any more than you do, maybe less, havin' had his skulduggery rubbed in my face for years now. But my duty——"

At the door of Clem Moon's office Clayburn turned angrily on his old friend. They could hear the subdued murmur of voices inside. Kruze and Moon were talking over bank business.

"Sheriff," Clayburn whispered patiently, "you got my word I won't start anything. But I won't be caught with empty holsters."

Algar shouldered the young Broken Key ramrod to one side and reached for the knob.

"I'll go in first," he said, "and I'll keep an eye on Kruze the whole time. But I can't arrest him for Weber's murder without a warrant, an' that'll take Randie's signature——"

Clayburn sucked in a deep breath as he saw Algar shove Moon's door open without the formality of a knock.

Kyle Kruze was standing before the big desk where Clem Moon was seated with a dossier of papers spread out before him.

Wheeling to face Algar and Clayburn, Kyle Kruze instinctively brought his arms upward, reading the menace in their faces.

"Clayburn," the Wagonspoke gambler said in a gusty voice, "it was not necessary to bring Algar here. I am bowing to your ultimatum to leave the town."

216

Tuck scowled, sensing treachery in Kruze's words.

"You're leaving?"

"As soon as I can put my affairs in order. Moon here will continue to operate the bank. I will probably sell out to financial interests in San Francisco or Los Angeles, as soon as it can be arranged."

Clayburn and Algar exchanged glances. The sheriff slowly relaxed his grip on his ivory gunstocks.

"About Broken Key," Clayburn said warily. "Who takes over the ranch when you pull stakes, Kruze?"

It was Kruze's turn to show a puzzled incomprehension. He turned to glance at Clem Moon. Tuck, following that glance, saw the old banker's face break into a grin.

"Why," Moon choked out incredulously, "Tuck doesn't know. He hasn't seen Garbie since he got back to town!"

Tuck blinked. "Don't know what, Clem?"

Clem fished through his papers on the desk and drew forth a folded sheet of yellow paper. It was an Overland Telegraph flimsy. Without speaking, Moon held out the telegram.

Walking past Algar, sensing some drama in the situation which up to now had escaped him, Tuck Clayburn reached for the paper. The writing blurred together, making no immediate sense to him:

GABRIEL GARBIE,
c/o VALLEY MERCANTILE,
WAGONSPOKE, CALIF.
    HERD DEL . . .

Stamped in bright red ink across the face of the telegraph form was the Wagonspoke operator's explanation for the un-

217

completed message: *TRANSMISSION INTERRUPTED 11:27 AM.*

Tuck looked up at Moon.

"Then this means—"

The banker flashed an exultant look at Kyle Kruze.

"It means Kyle didn't sink his hooks into Broken Key, Tuck. Garbie got enough of your message before the line went out to figure out that you had completed your deal with Kaploon."

Tuck stammered incoherently, "So you——"

"Garbie sent for me at a quarter to twelve yesterday morning," Moon said. "Within five minutes after that I was depositing a hundred thousand in cash to Broken Key's account. When Kruze showed up last night I presented him with Fred's notes, paid in full with accrued compound interest."

The telegraph flimsy fluttered from Tuck's nerveless hands. He turned to stare accusingly at Algar.

"Did you know this—and didn't tell Randie?"

The sheriff shook his head. "I ain't talked to Garbie or Moon in days, son. All I knew was that Kyle Kruze asked the protection of the law."

Clayburn turned to Kruze. The gambler remained where he had been standing since their entry to the bank office.

Kruze licked his lips.

"I guess," he said in a rattly whisper, "that this cleans up our personal accounts, Tuck."

Clayburn's glance shuttled over to the sheriff, then back to Kruze.

"I'm not so sure, Kruze. You've overlooked something."

Kruze's hands clenched, his eyes taking on a wild glare.

218

"Randie saw you shoot Cloyd Weber in the back, Kruze. You won't be leaving Verde Valley after all. You're going to hang for murdering that lawyer up in South Canyon the other day. That's why the sheriff's with me."

Kruze's swarthy face went slack and colorless. He half turned, caught sight of the tail-end of Arnie Algar's movement as he pulled a pair of handcuffs out of his hip pocket.

Algar started to say something, but whatever it was never reached his lips.

Dropping into a gunman's crouch, Kyle Kruze flicked his extended arms in a twitching motion and as if by magic the glittering black snouts of concealed .41 derringers appeared in his fists.

The hide-out guns were coming up, covering Algar and Tuck Clayburn in deftly-executed simultaneous drops, when Tuck Clayburn's hand slapped his gun-stock.

As he had done in facing Trig McCoy, the Broken Key man made no attempt to draw his Colt. His holster swiveled on his belt and he squeezed trigger when the gun came level, his bullet streaking its sightless path above the papers on Clem Moon's desk and slamming Kruze's chest with a meaty, slapping impact.

Through blossoming gunsmoke Clayburn saw Kruze's sleeve guns spit their needles of purple-orange fire, but his hands were already dropping and the .41 slugs smashed into the rug at his feet.

Across the room, Sheriff Algar's big .44 thundered. The crashing jolt of his fast-triggered lead smashed Kruze's toppling body. It dropped heavily against Moon's desk before crumpling into a shapeless mass on the floor.

All this had transpired between two ticks of the ornate

clock on the wall behind Clem Moon's chair. The banker came unsteadily to his feet and peered over his desk.

Kruze's leonine head was slumped against his chest and his life blood was spilling like a red curtain over his contorted features.

Clayburn was on his way to the door when he turned to see Algar slowly holstering his guns.

"Tell Doc Ashton for me," the Broken Key puncher husked out. "I've got to get out to the ranch."

The sun was blotted out by lowering storm clouds and premature dusk was over the land when Tuck Clayburn swung down from his winded horse in front of the Broken Key bunkhouse.

He strode into the shack to find Ben Tweedy and Flapjack Farley and the rest of the despondent Broken Key crew heaping their warsacks on the floor.

"Kruze ain't sent anybody out to evict us yet, boss," Ben Tweedy greeted Clayburn. "Reckon he——"

"Our telegram got through to Garbie before Kruze cut the wires," Clayburn said. "We won't be leaving Broken Key, now or ever." He turned to head for the main house.

"Kruze," Clayburn said as an afterthought, "is dead."

The crew was massing in the bunkhouse door when Tuck Clayburn started toward the ranch house at a run. A heavy lightning flash put its green-gold glare over the mesa and before the following thunderclap came Tweedy shouted after the sprinting ramrod.

"Randie ain't in the house, kid. She's out there sayin' *adios* to ol' Fred an' Molly. You must o' missed her comin' past——"

Tuck Clayburn halted in his tracks, staring back at his crew for a moment before he understood what he had heard.

He turned then, starting out toward the cottonwood bosque at a brisk walk which turned into the awkward, stilted run of a man in tight-fitting cowboots.

He saw Randie at the graveyard gate, but an ear-riving thunderclap overhead drowned out his shout to her. But the urgency of it brought the girl out from under the trees, brought her running toward him as the first down-slashing whip of warm rain in four years assaulted the earth.

They met there as the storm's full fury broke around them, oblivious to the lancing rain and the yellow puddles forming at their feet, oblivious to all else but their own togetherness at the threshold of the long years lying ahead.

The rainstorm's streamers lowered, blotting out the lower valley and the cowtown and the distant mountains. Rocks and brush lost their veneer of dust and glistened wetly in the play of lightning.

Broken Key's fertile earth drank greedily of Nature's overdue cup, while far out above the crown of the Lava-stones the thunder drums hammered out their gladsome melody for Tuck and Randie, matching the wild tempo of their own hearts.

THE END

Walker A. Tompkins, known to fellow Western writers as "Two-Gun" because of the speed with which he wrote, was the creator of two series characters still fondly remembered, Tommy Rockford in Street and Smith's *Wild West Weekly* and the Paintin' Pistoleer in Dell Publishing's *Zane Grey's Western Magazine*. Tompkins was born in Prosser, Washington, and his memories of growing up in the Washington wheat country he later incorporated into one of his best novels, *West of Texas Law* (1948). He was living in Ocean Park, Washington in 1931 when he submitted his first story to Wild West Weekly. It was purchased and Tommy Rockford, first a railroad detective and later a captain with the Border Patrol, made his first appearance. Quite as popular was the series of White Wolf adventures he wrote for this magazine about Jim-Twin Allen under the house name **Hal Dunning**. During the Second World War Tompkins served as a U.S. Army correspondent in Europe. Of all he wrote for the magazine market after leaving the service, his series about Justin O. Smith, the painter in the little town of Apache who is also handy with a six-gun, proved the most popular and the first twelve of these stories were collected in *The Paintin' Pistoleer* (1949). Tompkins's Golden Age began with *Flaming Canyon* (1948) and extended through such titles as *Manhunt West* (1949), *Border Ambush* (1951), *Prairie Marshal* (1952) and *Gold on the Hoof* (1953). His Western fiction is known for its intriguing plots, vivid settings, memorable characters, and engaging style. When, later in life, he turned to writing local history about Santa Barbara where he lived, he was honored by the California State Legislature for his contributions.